**"If you're going to arrest me,
get it over with," June said.
"But I didn't kill him."**

She moved to push past the police officers that were blocking the door.

She didn't get far. Instead, Ray Taylor abruptly grabbed her shoulder and spun her into his arms, pressing her tightly against his chest. "Let it go, June. Stop fighting what you really feel."

June resisted him only a moment, then her body crumpled and she sank against him, wild sobs bursting from her as she clenched his shirt in both hands.

Books by Ramona Richards

Love Inspired Suspense

A Murder Among Friends
The Face of Deceit
The Taking of Carly Bradford
Field of Danger
House of Secrets

RAMONA RICHARDS

A writer and editor since 1975, Ramona Richards has worked on staff with a number of publishers. Ramona has also freelanced with more than twenty magazine and book publishers and has won awards for both her fiction and nonfiction. She's written everything from sales-training video scripts to book reviews, and her latest articles have appeared in *Today's Christian Woman, College Bound* and *Special Ed Today.* She sold a story about her daughter to *Chicken Soup for the Caregiver's Soul,* and *Secrets of Confidence,* a book of devotionals, is available from Barbour Publishing.

In 2004, the God Allows U-Turns Foundation, in conjunction with the Advanced Writers and Speakers Association (AWSA), chose Ramona for their "Strength of Choice" award, and in 2003, AWSA nominated Ramona for Best Fiction Editor of the Year. The Evangelical Press Association presented her with an award for reporting in 2003, and in 1989 she won the Bronze Award for Best Original Dramatic Screenplay at the Houston International Film Festival. A member of the American Christian Fiction Writers and the Romance Writers of America, she has five other novels complete or in development.

HOUSE OF SECRETS

Ramona Richards

Love Inspired

™ LOVE INSPIRED BOOKS

ISBN-13: 978-0-373-44439-7

HOUSE OF SECRETS

www.LoveInspiredBooks.com

Printed in U.S.A.

For you did not receive the spirit of bondage
again to fear, but you received the
Spirit of adoption by whom we cry out,
"Abba, Father." The Spirit Himself bears witness
with our spirit that we are children of God.
—*Romans* 8: 15-16

This one is for Diane, Krista, Jessica,
Emily and Tina, with thanks, appreciation
and gratitude for your intelligence,
guidance and support through it all.
Y'all are a true blessing in my life.

ONE

"I did not kill Pastor David."

June Presley Eaton tried to swallow her fear as well as the lump of grief in her throat. Her upraised hands trembled, and she felt the phone clutched in her left hand slip slightly. *I have to maintain control.* June lifted both hands a bit higher and forced her voice lower. "I found him. I wanted to help," she said to the man standing behind her.

Please, Lord, let him believe me. It was a desperate prayer, and June fought a tightening sense of panic. She had a dead pastor lying at her feet and, she was pretty certain, Sheriff Ray Taylor and his deputies at her back, guns drawn. Without turning, June wagged the cordless phone in her hand. From it, the flattened and tinny screeches of the Bell County dispatcher bounced off the kitchen walls of the Victorian parsonage.

"June Presley Eaton! Is that you? Don't tell me you decided to upset Pastor David right before his big event! Someone already heard the fight and called us and Ray is on his way right now, and—"

June hit the off button with her thumb. "I just got here, Ray. I wasn't the one fighting with him. There are footprints leading farther into the house. See them? And when I got here, I could still hear someone back there." The lump in her throat had eased, but the fear still bore into her, tensing every muscle in her lower back and sending a shudder up her spine. *Please, Lord.*

No response came from the sheriff, however, and in the silence that followed, June knew that all of Ray's instincts had kicked into gear. His brown eyes scanning the room, he'd assess the scene in front of him with that precise, military-trained way he had of observing everything quickly before making a judgment. He would calmly evaluate the crime scene while she stood over a dead body, covered in blood, hands raised, cops clustered at her back with their guns pointing at her. June knew that only the phone in her hand kept her from looking like a suspect. She closed her eyes, praying that Ray would see the same thing she had as she'd approached the broad back porch of the White Hills Gospel Immanuel Chapel's parsonage: bloody footprints leading away from the door and out into the yard.

That had been her cue to fly into the house, calling David Gallagher's name. June had entered the kitchen, moving fast, and her sneakers had hit the red pool gathering around David's body before she could stop. She'd skidded and fallen forward, hitting the floor with a painful thud, her hands splashing down on either side of the butcher knife protruding from David's ribs.

Even during her years as a street kid, she'd never come face-to-face with violence like this.

Once June had stopped screaming, she'd scrambled to her feet and lunged for the phone, barely having time to dial 911 before the screen door had banged open and Ray's command to "Freeze!" had brought everything to a standstill.

In the silence, a fly buzzed around her blood-coated right hand. Trying to look over her shoulder, June struggled to speak in a quieter tone. *Control. Stay in control.* "Please, Ray. I'm a witness, not a suspect." She took another deep breath, working to sound much more dignified than she felt. "And please close that door. You're letting the flies into the house."

No one moved. Then, after a few seconds that felt like at least a decade, Ray spoke, his baritone voice even and thoroughly professional. "Rivers. Gage. Clear the house."

Silently, Ray's deputies, Daniel Rivers and Jeff Gage, moved through the kitchen and past June and the pastor's body into the main areas of the grand old Victorian. Over the next few minutes, their calls of "Clear!" echoed through the rooms.

"Can I at least put my arms down?"

"Why are you here, June?"

"I came to confront David about what he'd said—" She broke off, suddenly realizing how suspicious *that* sounded.

"About what?" Ray's tone grew more agitated as he holstered his gun, stepped over David's legs and moved in front of her. "What did you need to confront him about?"

June straightened her back and took the holstered gun for a sign she could lower her arms. "What he said yesterday morning from the pulpit."

The tension in Ray's voice revealed his impatience. "About *what?*"

"Hunter Bridges."

Silence reigned in the room again as Ray simply waited, eyes dark and demanding.

June's hands suddenly shook at her sides, and she looked around for a place to put the phone, her words picking up speed. "Hunter Bridges is a canker sore on the face of this town and you know it. I don't care how much David wants to see him in the state senate. He's a lying, manipulative, womanizing cheat, and I don't want him representing me or to have my name connected to his." She lowered her voice. "I've witnessed his ability to manipulate people to get what he wants. He's propositioned two married friends of mine. I'm done with him." With no flat surface close enough, the phone grew awkward in her hand. A wicked pain snapped through her head, making her grimace. "David's implied before that I support Hunter, and I've politely asked him not to. He did it again yesterday morning, in front of the whole church, and I knew polite just wasn't going to cut it anymore."

"So you were here to yell at him. You were mad."

"Well, yes! I won't have my name mixed up with that no-good politician Hunter Bridges." She threw up a hand in front of her face, then stopped, taking a deep breath to calm down. "But I was too late. When I got here, I saw the bloody footprints on the porch and I ran in. I slipped…" She paused, pointing down at the floor. "I fell."

"Is that why you're covered in his blood?"

She nodded.

Ray's gaze held an intensity that aggravated her growing sense of panic. "But you didn't kill him."

June's knees began trembling, and she fought the urge to throw the phone at him. *He's just doing his job. Don't lose it!* "No, I did *not* kill him. David and I have been disagreeing about Hunter Bridges for weeks. We've debated over coffee, over lunch. He wouldn't give up trying to convince me. He thought Hunter had great things ahead of him. I think Hunter should be locked in his office and kept away from sharp objects."

She shook her head and pointed at a stack of flyers lying on the kitchen counter. "I don't know why David suddenly wanted to be politically active. He never had before. I thought he followed JR's philosophy of keeping politics out of the church. But that's his business. Then he started in on me to support Hunter because, for some unfathomable reason, he thinks people in this county still listen to me. I warned him that if he didn't stop, I was going to take out a full-page ad in the paper explaining exactly what I thought of Hunter Bridges, his career and his mother. David thought I was stubborn, and I thought him politically naive. That may be grounds for an argument, but not murder."

"Wasn't David hosting a political dinner tomorrow night?"

"Yes, and he invited me. But I told him I'd rather chew glass. You know I don't like mixing politics with religion any more than JR did."

The pain spiked under her scalp at the mention of her dead husband, and June pressed her palm to her forehead, trying to push the headache away. Her whole body seemed to quiver now. Even her voice held a tremor, and tears abruptly stung her eyes. "You know how hard JR worked to keep politics out of the church."

Ray's low voice turned gentle. "Yes. Everyone knows."

June took a deep, ragged breath and closed her eyes, trying to stave off the tears. *Of course everyone knows. David, why didn't you follow his guidance? After three years, what changed?* June tried to push away a sudden flood of memories of JR, from their wedding day in a tiny mountain chapel to the instant a heart attack took him from her—and the entire congregation.

"Come back to me, June," Ray urged. "Don't retreat from this. Stay in control." Ray's soft bass tones resonated in an almost comforting way. "You've been trembling like a leaf since I walked in, and you're about to have the worst adrenaline headache of your life, if you don't already. But you have to hang on to it, girl. We'll get through this. *I'll* get you through it."

June stared down at her hands. The red had darkened, the blood turning brownish as it dried. Suddenly, a foul scent from David's body reached her and June realized it must have been there all along. Her entire body shook, and the impact of the situation hit her anew. *David's dead. Murdered. No wonder I'm babbling like an idiot. Lord, I need calm. And I need Your strength.*

Nodding, she looked back up at Ray and let out the breath she'd been holding. "You know I didn't do this."

"We have to clear you with evidence before I can let you go." His dark eyes shifted as he looked behind her, and she turned toward Rivers and Gage, who both shook their heads.

"Nothing," said Rivers. "All clear, although the study has been partially ransacked. Looks like the search might have been interrupted, but if anyone was here, he's long gone."

June shook her head. "I know he was still here. I could hear him in the study. Did you check the tunnel?"

The three men stared at June, and Ray stiffened. "What tunnel?"

Ray held the flashlight in his left hand, shoulder level and pointed slightly down. The earthen tunnel in front of him soaked up the light, and the air smelled acrid and moldy, reminding Ray of a flooded riverbank after a hard rain. Ray ran the beam of his light back and forth across the floor of the narrow tunnel. Behind him, his chief deputy, Daniel Rivers, searched the walls.

Daniel paused to examine a lump, which turned out to be the end of a tree root. "I can't believe there's a tunnel under the parsonage."

"By now, I suspect we're out under the backyard. A lot of houses this old have secret rooms and passages, but not usually tunnels."

"An escape route for slaves, maybe?"

Ray paused and ran his light over one of the wooden support arches to check its strength. "I doubt it. This house wasn't built until around 1900. June told me once that the original builder had been seriously paranoid about fire. Since the only entrance is from the second floor, I'd say he built it from a fear of fire or intruders."

Daniel cleared his throat. "You think she did it?"

Ray, trying desperately to forget the feelings he had for his number-one suspect, resumed his examination of the floor. "She's your sister-in-law. What do you think?"

Daniel, who'd married June's sister April less than a year ago, paused a moment. "No."

"Why not?"

"June likes a good argument, and she likes to win, but she's worked hard over the years to leave behind the street kid that she was. She wouldn't resort to violence. She's so in control most days, I forget she's not from a privileged background. April once said June lived with violence so long that she abhorred it. They both do. June might yell, but she'd never lift a hand to hurt anyone." Daniel sniffed, then coughed. "Besides, she kept referring to Pastor Gallagher in the present tense, as if he were still alive. Plus, the blood pattern on her clothes is all wrong."

Ray smiled grimly, glad Daniel couldn't see the flash of pride in his face. Daniel got better at his job every day. "How so?"

"The killer would have blood on him in streaks and smudges from the attack. June looked like she'd wallowed in it. Plus the footprints on the back porch don't match the ones that skidded through the blood. So there were at least two people in that kitchen. June and whoever made the prints."

"Maybe three, if the set leading away from—" Ray froze, his light focused on something on the ground.

Daniel came to his side, on alert. "What did you find?"

Ray nodded toward the floor, then they both squatted, examining the small white button that seemed to glitter in the light. A tiny piece of navy-blue fabric still clung to it, and both had a distinctive red smear on them.

"Strange place to lose a button."

Ray shined his light farther down the tunnel, where it illuminated a pile of plaid cloth. Red streaks had soaked the navy-blue and dark green squares. "Not if you were jerking your shirt off."

Daniel stood. "I'll send Gage down with the crime-scene kit."

"Good."

Ray pulled his handcuffs from his belt and placed them carefully next to the button, so it would be easier to find. Standing, he shined his light back toward the house, noticing how distinct his and Daniel's footprints were in the earth. He noticed other prints that seemed recent as well, and he skirted them as he turned back and made his way deeper into the tunnel, toward the shirt.

Using his pen, Ray prodded at the thick flannel until he found the collar. The shirt was a man's extra large, which made it useless for judging the suspect's size. Small shirts are only worn by small people, but large shirts are popular with all sizes of folks. The dirt ring around the collar meant that the shirt could be old—and filled with DNA. Two dark smears on the cloth bore an unmistakable resemblance to tobacco juice.

Ray replaced the pen in his pocket and stood again, his mind turning over a hundred possibilities. He ignored the relief he felt at finding some possible evidence that pointed away from June. Tobacco stains didn't exactly narrow the suspect pool much—Bell County remained tobacco country and there were as many fields of the bright, wide-leafed plants around here as there were of corn and soybeans—but it might not be a bad place to start looking. Especially if it could help clear the name of the woman he could not get off his mind. The woman who just wanted to be "friends."

The scuff of shoes on dirt made Ray look up, and he shined his light down the tunnel behind him, expecting to see Daniel and his lone crime-scene investigator, Jeff Gage, heading his way. Instead, the beam of his flashlight faded away into the darkness.

Then the scuffing sounded again, now clearly from the opposite direction. Ray drew his pistol and swung around, dropping to a crouch.

* * *

June perched on the outside edge of the carefully placed kitchen chair, tense and weary. Her foot bounced nervously, the white crime-scene suit she now wore crinkling and crunching with every movement. Before he and Daniel had headed off to explore the tunnel, Ray had given her the suit and insisted she exchange her bloody clothes for the Tyvek coverall. He also pulled a chair from the far side of the room and told her to sit there once her clothes were in evidence bags. He placed it where every officer on the premises could see her. For her safety, he'd said.

She could see them as well. She watched as Jeff Gage went to his patrol cruiser and returned with the crime-scene kit, beginning his work on the body. Photographs, diagrams and evidence bags. He'd placed brown paper bags around David's hands, and for the first time June saw the defensive wounds on her pastor's arms.

You fought back. Good for you. Tears stung June's eyes again as she realized that there was no forced entry. David must have let them in—he must have known his attackers. Her stomach knotted as a sense of betrayal shot through her. *How could anyone…?* June pressed her fingers to her lips, fighting a wave of grief.

When JR first took over here at Gospel Immanuel Chapel in tiny White Hills, Tennessee, the congregation had barcly numbered one hundred. She and JR had worked hard to build the church, and within a year, JR had needed an assistant and an associate pastor. He'd hired Kitty Parker as his assistant and David Gallagher as his associate pastor, for his knowledge of scripture, charisma in the pulpit and genuine love of people. After JR's death, David became the senior pastor. Over the past three years of his tenure in that role, David had grown the church even more, and he knew every member by name and their problems and their hopes.

June shifted in her chair, her heart aching for David. *You were a good shepherd. Did you know them? Were they friends?*

David had either let his attacker in…or the killer had come in through the tunnel.

Not many folks knew about that underground passageway in and out of the house. In fact, when she and JR had started the renovation of the parsonage the year before he'd died, the entrance on the second floor had been sealed. The contractor told her it had probably been closed off for at least twenty years, since the house had been empty for more than ten years. And the previous owners had known nothing about a tunnel.

JR had found the tunnel fascinating, even though the dark passageway was little more than a deep ditch that had been covered over with railroad ties and sod. It let out at the spring house. Although deep enough for a man to stand up in, only two feet or so of dirt and wood separated it from the expanse of grass that grew fresh and even across the backyard. JR had insisted on having the tunnel inspected for safety. They'd never really used it except for the time they had left the house that way in order to sneak away undetected by the neighbors for a romantic three days in Gulf Shores. A pretend adventure that still made June smile.

A rhythmic thudding on the main stairway of the house made June turn, and she stood as Daniel entered the kitchen. "Where's Ray?"

"Still down there." He motioned for Gage to follow him. "Bring your kit."

"What did you find?" June asked, taking a step toward her brother-in-law.

"Later. Stay here." He waited as Gage repacked the kit. As they turned to go, two muffled thumps echoed from somewhere deep in the house. They looked at each other, puzzled, as two more thumps sounded, like a car backfiring in some far distant place.

Gage recognized it first. "That's gunfire!"

TWO

Ray Taylor's ears rang, and his head throbbed with an almost blinding pain. Blue and white dots danced angrily before his eyes, and a spreading dampness on the left side of his skull slid through his hair and down his neck. Ray clenched his jaw and sank heavily against the wall of the tunnel, sliding to a sitting position.

When he'd swung around, only his instinct to crouch and weave to the right had kept him alive. A bright spotlight flashed suddenly, blinding him, and one of the shots that followed went wild, while the other grazed the left side of his head instead of hitting him square in the chest. He'd returned two quick shots, and the intruder had dropped the spotlight and fled out of the tunnel. The bouncing stream of light from the abandoned spot had illuminated the attacker's path out of the tunnel but nothing about his identity. Definitely a man, a slender, wiry one, but otherwise Ray had seen only shadows among the flashing dots in his eyes.

He pressed his left hand against his wound and took two deep breaths, holding each for several seconds before releasing them slowly. His right hand still held his pistol in a crushing grip, but both hands now shook furiously. Adrenaline seared through him, and anger that he had not been able to follow the intruder made his stomach roil. But blinded, deafened by gunshots and bleeding, Ray knew he'd be more of a target than aggressor. He tried to radio Daniel, but the signal wouldn't penetrate the earth and wood overhead.

Ray squeezed his eyes tightly shut, waiting for the blue and white sparks to dissipate and his ears to clear. As they did, he could hear the frantic thuds of shoes on the narrow ladder leading from the parsonage's second floor. Hidden behind a sliding panel in one of the hallway closets, the solid wooden ladder had been built into one side of a thin shaft between the walls, exiting into the tunnel through the home's foundation.

One by one, five of his officers cleared the ladder and rushed in his direction, led by Daniel Rivers. The streams of gold from their flashlights bounced around the tunnel like out-of-control basketballs. "Slow down!" Ray commanded.

Daniel reached him first, shining his light on Ray's head. "What happened?" he asked, digging a handkerchief out of his pocket. He peeled Ray's hand away from the wound and pressed the cloth tightly against it.

Ray filled them in, then instructed Gage and the others to continue the search down the tunnel. He pointed at the big handheld spot, which still shined its penetrating light down the tunnel. "Use gloves. Take that with you. He's long gone now, but go slow. Look for any sign that I hit the guy."

As they moved away and the light dimmed, Ray took the cloth from Daniel, folded it into a neater square and pressed it to his head again. Daniel watched his boss's face a moment, then said quietly, "What are you thinking?"

Ray holstered his gun, then pushed himself to his feet with his free hand. Daniel steadied his off-balance sheriff with a hand on one arm.

Ray nodded his thanks, then checked the handkerchief to see if his bleeding had stopped. His head still throbbed from the blow, and he squinted from the pain. His mind, however, spun furiously with his recall of the past few minutes.

Demonstrating his attacker's actions, he held his right hand at shoulder level. "He held the light here, out to the side and pointed down. If I hadn't ducked, the shots would have hit me square in the chest. A fraction more to the right, and this one would have knocked me out, at the very least. I don't think he expected me to survive, much less return fire. I fired to the left of the light and hit nothing. When I fired right at it, he dropped it and ran, probably realizing that the shots would bring you guys running."

"So you think he's a pro?"

"Or a former cop. At least he's someone who's pretty good at his job. And there's a good chance he's left-handed."

Daniel nodded. "The knife entered the right side of David's body, low, an upward thrust."

Ray pressed his fingers to his skull again, and they came away only slightly sticky. "That's a combat move. Misses the ribs and goes straight to the heart."

"But to complete that move, wouldn't he have twisted the knife and pulled it back out? Why didn't he take the knife?"

Ray shook his head. "I thought about that. Not sure. But I bet we don't find any prints." He gestured down the tunnel. "My guess is that's our killer."

"So David lets him in—or maybe them—in the back door because he knows them. They kill him, but then they hear June drive up. You know that old Corvette of hers needs a new muffler."

"And a transmission."

Ray went on, his words picking up speed. "One takes off across the yard, while the other one heads down here, giving himself more time to get away. If a pro had to run, he may have not wanted to take a chance of getting caught with the knife."

"So you're convinced this wasn't a botched robbery or home invasion."

Ray shook his head. "Whoever it was came specifically to kill David Gallagher."

"He just didn't expect June to show up."

Ray nodded. "She made him get sloppy." He paused. "You *did* send someone to the other end of the tunnel?"

"The minute we heard the shots. June told us the

tunnel came out at the spring house. I sent the rest of the crew there. Carter was already out in the crowd out front, so I put him on point."

Ray scowled. "Who's watching June? She's still officially a suspect."

Daniel glanced down, his lips twitching slightly. "The coroner was there, but I…uh…I handcuffed her to the kitchen cabinet in case the coroner needed to leave."

Ray's eyebrows arched as an image of exactly how well that idea must have gone over flashed through his mind. "I'm glad *you're* the one married to her sister."

"Well…"

"Well, what?"

"The handcuffs weren't just to keep her away from the evidence. They were to keep her from coming down here. She heard the shots and took off for that ladder. I almost had to tackle her to keep her out of here."

Ray stared at his young deputy. His racing thoughts stalled for the first time as conflicting emotions and images swirled through his head and heart. June, his suspect—his lovely, brown-haired, blue-eyed suspect—had stood terrified and trembling over David's body. Yet when gunshots rang out, her instinct had been to run *toward* him…and into potential danger. *What is going on with her?*

Ray wrestled his thoughts about June aside, his mouth tightening into a thin line. "Let's go upstairs and soothe the ruffled feathers."

"You need a doctor for that wound."

Ray turned and headed toward the ladder. "I'm not dying. First things first. Let's clear the crime scene, then I'll go over and have them stitch this up."

They headed upstairs to find that the kitchen held only the coroner and her assistant. A pair of handcuffs dangled from one cabinet's door handle. Ray glared at Daniel, who said weakly, "We have her car blocked in. She couldn't have gone very far."

"June!" Ray bellowed suddenly, almost amused at how Daniel jumped.

"What?"

The quiet question came from behind them, and they turned to see June, wiping her hands on a small towel.

Ray's eyes narrowed. "How did you—"

"Why are you bleeding?" June stared at the side of his head. "Did you get shot?"

"I'm fine. Answer my question."

"You're not fine. You have a hole in the side of your skull. Being a Marine doesn't mean you're invincible, you know." She reached for Ray, but he caught her wrist.

"Just answer the question."

Relenting, June rolled her eyes as she pulled her hand away. She turned and pointed at Daniel. "You. You should never handcuff anyone next to a drawer full of tools." She looked back at Ray. "Don't have a fit. Your deputies wouldn't let me go to the tunnel, and standing there handcuffed to the cabinet was distinctly undignified."

When Ray continued to stare, unmoving, June gave in with a soft sigh. "Okay, I had to go to the ladies' room before things got dire. And it wasn't easy in this suit." She plucked at the arm of the white coverall.

"You washed your hands."

She nodded. "I only touched the floor and the phone, Ray. No evidence at all on my hands."

"Unless you killed him."

"Well, if I did, then your deputy is going to have to find a new career, isn't he?" she said with a forced smile.

There was a false lightness in June's voice that worried Ray. He wondered if being handcuffed might have pushed her into her dark past, dredging up memories she'd do anything to avoid. Ray moved closer to her. "Are you okay, June? I feel like I'm losing you a little. Is there anything you want to tell me?" He looked at her, hard.

June stilled, her deep blue eyes narrowing as she searched his face, her skin losing its color again, stark against her dark brown hair. When she spoke, her words were flat and void of emotion.

"If you're going to arrest me, get it over with, Ray. But I didn't kill him." She pushed past the two men blocking the door.

She didn't get far. Instead, Ray Taylor abruptly grabbed her shoulder and spun her around. "June, I wish I could just let you walk right out of here, but you know I can't. Now sit back down in that chair or I'm going to have Rivers handcuff you again."

And then June did something that surprised everyone, especially Ray.

She burst into tears.

THREE

June wiped her face on the same towel she'd dried her hands on only ten minutes before. She perched on her kitchen chair again, a headache slowly but steadily circling her skull with pain. She clutched the towel, looking for some kind of reassurance, but her mind was flooded with memories. Seeing David's dead body brought back the horror of being fourteen and watching her father beat her mother halfway to death. She had been sprawled out at June's feet, so still June had thought her dead. Three years later, she would be. June's father had kicked June out of the house the day her mother died, forcing her to live on the street.

Memories of her parents gave way to visions of her brother Marc, just thirteen, his face raw with wounds and gray in death. And her sisters, bruised and terrified, huddling away from the rages of their father, a man who turned home into a horror house that had sent April into a brutal early marriage and June into the dark world of the streets. Only Lindsey, four years younger but somehow wiser, had conquered the terror. After their mother's death, she'd sued her father for emancipation at fifteen and won. Righteously angry at the world, Lindsey had walked away from her entire family. June had kept track of her on the internet, but neither she nor April had seen their sister since.

As June watched the coroner zip the body bag closed, she shook off one last memory: JR, three years ago, collapsed on the floor beside his pulpit, dead before he'd hit the floor from a heart attack so massive the doctors doubted he'd felt anything.

June forced herself to come back to the present. She looked around the room. Deputy Gage was finishing last-minute tasks with the crime-scene kit, pulling fingerprints from the kitchen table and labeling the last of the blood samples.

Standing in the hallway door, Ray and Daniel conferred over diagrams of the crime scene as the coroner and one of the deputies loaded Pastor David's body on the gurney and wheeled him out. Outside, dozens of faces peered intently, dodging back and forth, trying to get the best view through the door.

The parsonage, like the church itself, sat in the middle of one of White Hills' oldest and most established residential sections. One reason the Victorian had been the house of choice to replace the crumbling cottage where she and JR had first lived in this small town was its proximity to the church. It was literally next door, surrounded by the homes of potential members.

Members who now peered inside, desperate for more information. Tears coated the faces of most of the women and some of the men as the news about David spread. They held each other, some scared and anxious, others angry. They stared at her through the open door, sitting there in her white suit.

Guilty. They thought she was guilty.

June closed her eyes, memories again flashing through her mind. Other times that people stared and pointed. As JR was carried from the sanctuary. As her mother's body had been removed from their house.

The day she had been arrested.

June had traded the abuse of home for the violence of the streets. She'd lived in abandoned boxes or sometimes at missions, working hard-labor jobs. As a kid, she'd discovered she was good with computers, so she tried to practice her gift in libraries and friends' apartments whenever she could crash with someone, hoping it might help her get a job and get off the street somehow. And it did—in a way. An underground hacker discovered her talents, giving her a place to sleep while recruiting her to wreak mischief on corporations and local governments. She could defeat almost any firewall, break through almost any security system. And she'd loved it. Finally good at something, finally praised for her work, June took pride in tackling what she saw as the greatest puzzle-solving game ever.

When the police arrested her for computer crimes, June's world crashed. A year later, she was eighteen, on parole and back on the streets, broke and hopeless, ready to get back to hacking. Until the night she wandered into one of Jackie Rhea "JR" Eaton's mobile soup kitchens.

"June?"

She blinked up at Ray as if coming out of a dark dream.

"Are you okay?"

June pointed at her temple. "Headache."

Ray smiled wryly. "Yeah. No doubt."

The wound on his head had begun to bleed again, and June resisted the urge to reach toward it, to tend to him. "You ever going to the doctor with that? Seriously. You look awful." The coroner had cleaned his injury with a first-aid kit, putting on a temporary bandage, but dried blood still streaked his neck and matted his dark brown, closely cropped hair. Fresh blood discolored the bandage and tape.

"Thanks. You don't look much better yourself."

"No doubt," she replied, using one of Ray's favorite expressions. But she knew the truth as well. She'd skidded when she'd fallen and slipped twice trying to get up. Even with her washed hands and white suit, she had David's blood in her hair, which had to be topsy-turvy by now. And half of her makeup had shifted dramatically from its original location on her face.

"We still need to test your hair."

June's eyes widened in confusion. "I beg your pardon?"

"The blood. David fought back. Not a lot and not for long, but he could have injured one of his attackers. There may be blood from—"

"*One* of his attackers?"

Ray hesitated, then nodded. "You saw the footprints on the porch. So we think there were at least two. One went out the back, one through the tunnel. And maybe one of them left his blood here, too."

June understood where he was going. "And I might have landed in it as well."

"Another reason I didn't want you to wash your hands."

"Sorry."

"It's done. But I don't want to miss another chance. Can you ask April to pick up a change of clothes from your house and meet us at NorthCrest Medical?"

"Why do I need to go to NorthCrest?"

Ray shifted to stand squarely over both feet, then began counting off his reasoning. "A. Because you're covered in blood, possibly from more than one person. I want you on their records if something…untoward shows up in the blood work."

"You mean HIV."

"And hepatitis C. It's a precaution."

"I don't have any open—"

"B. Once the adrenaline subsides, you may find that you're really hurt somewhere. If you fell like you described, you hit pretty hard."

"Okay."

"And C. I'm not letting you out of my sight again until I get you to the station for a complete statement and someone is assigned to watch your house tonight."

June sat a bit straighter. "Watch my house? You think I'm in danger?"

Ray hesitated. "Depends on whether they believe you saw them leave."

"But I didn't—"

"You interrupted the search of the study. They have no idea what you saw. And you're still my material witness. Don't argue."

She stood up, stepping closer and tilting her head back to look up at his face. "What about my car? It has a tricky transmission."

"Everyone in the county knows your car has a tricky transmission. We'll leave it here for now. I'll send it home later with a guy who's good with a manual."

"You have to let it warm up at least ten minutes. Then make sure you put it in First before shifting to Reverse or it won't go anywhere. It has that 435-horsepower, big-block engine. You don't do it right, you'll leave half its innards sitting in the road."

"You should have that fixed."

"Yeah, but then it wouldn't be June's emerald-green 1968 Corvette with the tricky transmission."

"Notoriety isn't always a good thing."

"No such thing as bad publicity."

"Nothing good about being stranded on the side of the road."

"Not a bad way to meet new folks in a county like this."

"June." He took a step closer until they were toe to toe.

"What?"

"Get it fixed."

"So you won't worry about me?"

Ray's mouth tightened to a thin line, but his eyes glistened a bit. June wasn't sure if he was going to laugh or yell.

He yelled. But he never took his eyes off hers. "Rivers!"

Daniel came to his side and Ray stepped back from June. "Please call your wife and ask her to bring a change of clothes for June to NorthCrest. We'll be there in thirty minutes. Radio the station and the hospital that we're on our way."

"Yes, sir."

"And ask Carter to clear that crowd back from the house."

"Yes, sir."

Ray held out his hand. "June, I need your keys."

"They're in the ignition."

Ray's eyes narrowed. "You left the keys in a Corvette?"

"Everybody in the county knows my car, as you just said. Would *you* steal it?"

Ray didn't argue with her reasoning. "Considering what one of your favorite Sunday school country boys would do if they saw anyone but you driving it? No."

Ray took June by the arm to escort her out. She paused at the door, looking out at the faces of the crowd that had grown even larger. "This could get ugly," she whispered.

"I'll take care of it."

"I don't suppose you could tell them—"

"Not yet."

"Maybe I could just tell them that I only found—"

"June, don't talk."

June nodded, then took a deep breath. *It's not like I haven't made this walk before.* She pushed open the door and stepped out on the porch.

The murmurings started immediately, and June cringed as the words hit her ears. It was as if she'd betrayed them all. Ray walked beside her, waving back those who got too close.

By the time he closed the car door, shutting out the voices, tears traced down June's cheeks, grief building again within her, composure slipping away.

Ray yanked open the driver's door. He fastened his seat belt, then touched her arm gently. "We'll get through this; I promise."

"The glass house a pastor lives in doesn't just vanish when he dies." She twisted toward him, grief boiling over. "You have no idea what it's like! What this brings back. How this makes me—" Her voice broke, and she wiped away tears in furious frustration.

"It brings back JR. Your dad. And your arrest."

June squeezed her eyes shut. "How did you—?" She stopped, pressing her lips together. *Of course he knows. He's the sheriff.* She took a deep breath to staunch the tears.

Ray looked her over carefully. "Just so you know, June, no matter what we do, these people out here are going to think you're being treated with favoritism because you're Daniel's sister-in-law and JR's widow." He paused, easing the cruiser through the cluster of cars in the yard. "And my friend."

June faced forward, looking down at her lap again. "Friend."

"Friend," Ray repeated. "Your choice, if I remember. Now fasten your seat belt." He pulled out of the parsonage driveway and headed toward Highway 49, which would take them into Springfield.

For the next ten minutes, neither of them spoke. June stared out her window as Ray focused on maneuvering Highway 49's hills and curves, and her thoughts turned to prayers. *Lord, we're going to need You more than ever. You were there when JR died. Please, guide us now. Help us have strength, understanding…and a little common sense wouldn't hurt, either.*

She looked down at her fingers, twisting them around each other. The truth was, this also felt as if she were betraying JR as well. She and JR had worked hard to transform her from a parolee to an elegant preacher's wife. She'd studied etiquette and taken design classes. She'd practiced walking with grace in three-inch heels until her back hurt and her shoulders cramped. She'd read the Bible until she knew almost every book by heart. They'd never hidden her past from the church, but some of the folks within had never forgiven her or forgotten that they had a felon for a preacher's wife. Only the fact that she'd never once slipped up, maintaining her elegance and class, had kept her in their good graces.

Now that JR no longer stood as her protector, the rumor mill would run out of control.

God, You've forgiven me. Why can't they? Because of my disagreements with David?

David. Despite her quarrels with him, she had cared about David Gallagher, cared that he succeeded in the church she and her husband had built. For the past three years, she'd supported him, even though she'd pulled back from her activities in the church following JR's death. In fact, until this business about Hunter had come up between them, she'd thought they were friends. But she'd begun to feel as if he was turning the people in the church against her over Hunter Bridges. And today had probably sealed her fate with them.

Their comments had upset her, but now that she thought about it, the same people who whispered behind their hands today were the same ones who always had. That would never change, guilty or innocent, no matter how good or bad her behavior. In every church, there are folks who dislike the pastor's wife, even if they love the pastor. That was the way of the world. But June had always refused to "court" them. She preferred being straightforward and honest, even if it came with a few bumps.

Or hurt someone.

She turned to look at Ray. Since JR's death, June hadn't considered dating. Ray had always been good to her, checking on her, making a few repairs around the house. But he'd never so much as suggested anything more. Until about six weeks ago, when he changed where he sat every Sunday at church.

He'd moved from the balcony to sit in her pew, five rows from the front. Even in a large church like Gospel Immanuel, everyone notices when the county sheriff starts sitting with the former preacher's wife. By the end of that first service, the rumor mill had already ground out its first tidbits. So she'd made it clear quickly: they were just friends. Nothing more.

She'd made it clear despite any feelings she had to the contrary, feelings she wasn't even ready to admit to herself, yet.

Ray had agreed. But he hadn't gone back to the balcony. And the man who was considered the best Bell County sheriff in its history had taken some hits to his reputation and authority. All because he'd chosen her as his friend.

She studied him now. His eyes, shadowed by physical pain, seemed to gaze into some far distance.

"I didn't mean to hurt you."

Ray blinked twice, as if she'd interrupted a major train of thought. "What?"

"By saying we were just friends."

He kept his eyes on the road as he slowly smiled. "June. All the best relationships start as friends."

Now it was her turn to blink in confusion. "Relationsh—"

An explosive pop cut off her words, and the cruiser jerked suddenly to the left, into oncoming traffic. June's seat belt wrenched her back against the seat, locking into place as Ray hit the brakes. He wrestled the car back to the right lane and slowed, the left front tire thudding heavily on the pavement.

He eased the car off onto the shoulder, out of all traffic, and turned on the blue lights on the roof. Letting out a long sigh, he looked at June.

"You okay?"

She nodded. "Although I didn't really need a second adrenaline rush today."

"No doubt." Ray reached for the radio and reported to the dispatcher what had happened, along with their location.

June looked around, realizing that while they weren't far from Springfield, they were still surrounded by farm country. Her window overlooked a steep embankment that led down to a stream. Beyond the stream the land rose and fell in the typical undulating nature of this part of Tennessee, and rows of soybeans fluttered in a light breeze.

As he replaced the radio, he reached for the door handle. "Stay put. I'll check on the tire."

At that moment, the window above Ray's hand cracked, and the radio exploded into tiny pieces as a bullet tore into it. Ray's shouts to get out of the car sounded muffled, until June realized they were being drowned out by her own frantic screams. Ray released her belt, pushing her toward the passenger door. June jerked on the handle and scrambled out just as the windshield in front of them spiderwebbed into a thousand shards.

June bent to squat down against the car but she fell, slamming into the door. Ray tried to hold on to her, but his grip slipped. Terror washed over her as she began to slide down the embankment.

FOUR

June's head cracked against a rock on the edge of the ravine and she went silent as she tumbled over. Scrambling but still trying to hold on to the car door, Ray frantically snatched at her arm but missed, and she slid away into the ravine. Ray let go of the door, dropping out of the line of fire and sliding down the rock-lined slope. He stumbled on the rock bed at the bottom, twisting his right ankle and hitting the ground hard. The rocks had punctured deep gashes in his right arm, but he clambered to June's side, calling her name and checking her pulse.

June, limp, pale and unconscious, had a deep cut on her forehead and abrasions on her right cheek and arms. Blood streamed down her face and Ray pulled his shirt open and ripped away part of his undershirt, pressing it hard against her forehead. Her pulse felt thready and uneven, and Ray yanked his cell phone from his pocket.

As he called into the station for backup and an ambulance, Ray drew in several deep gulps of air to steady his voice—and his nerves. Flipping the phone shut, he pressed the cloth against June's face again, then turned his attention up the ravine's bank. Using the cruiser for cover, he climbed the embankment slowly, ignoring the increased throbbing in his head and arm.

Peering around the rear tire, Ray spotted the assailant on the foliage-covered hillside that rose steeply away from the other side of the road. The yellow-white late-morning sunlight glinted off the grille of an SUV—and a rifle barrel. About ten yards below the rise of the hill, and camouflaged by thick brush, the sniper still sat, apparently waiting to make sure they had not survived.

"How did you get here so fast?" Ray muttered under his breath as he pulled his pistol from its holster. Bracing his arms, Ray took careful aim and fired three times.

The rifle went airborne with the first shot, and the assailant—a slender, wiry white man with dark, shaggy hair—scrambled after it. Ray could hear the raw, explosive words that burst from the gunman. The second and third shots shattered one headlight and the grille on the SUV and, Ray hoped, the radiator.

The assailant clawed the SUV's door open and slammed the vehicle into Reverse as Ray fired again, aiming for but missing the windshield. The SUV roared away as sirens filled the air, and Ray lowered his gun, sliding back down into the ravine toward June.

Pressing the cloth against her head again, Ray checked her pulse. Weak, and her breathing was shallow and slow. All his training, all his knowledge, fought desperately with his urge to gather her up in his arms and clutch her to his chest.

Instead, Ray clenched one fist at his side and waited for the sirens to close in, for the first responders who could truly rescue this woman. And in his mind he made plans for the man who'd tried to kill her.

"Where is she?" Ray winced as Fran Woodard cut his sleeve and peeled the cloth away from the gash on his left forearm, and the demanding tone in his voice lessened. "Who's seeing her?"

As a nurse, Fran had been taking care of Bell County's law enforcement officers since long before Ray had been on the force. Her hands were always firm but gentle, and her straightforward manner kept any attitude in line. She'd already cleaned and rebandaged the gunshot wound on the side of his head, and now she used a dampened gauze pad to loosen a bit of cloth stuck to his arm by clotted blood.

Ray sat on the bed in the E.R., his arm resting on one end of a rolling table, Fran's tray of supplies on the other. She picked up a cleansing antiseptic to use on the gash. "We're seeing too much of you boys lately. You need to be more careful." Fran clucked her tongue at him. "Stop fretting and sit still. Dr. Collins is in with her right now. The X-rays are back."

"Is she still unconscious?"

"Last I heard, she was awake and being stubborn about treatment."

Ray's quick grin shifted to a grimace as Fran began to clean the wound. "That's a good sign."

Fran shrugged. "Maybe. She needs to rest, not resist."

"Not June's style."

"Yeah, well, she won't have much choice if Dr. Collins decides to keep her overnight. That was quite a knock on her head."

Ray took a deep breath and steeled himself as Fran reached for tweezers.

"Hold still. You've just got a couple of pieces of gravel embedded."

Ray didn't want to close his eyes, even against the pain. Every time he did, he replayed the scenes from the shootings. "How did he get there so fast?" Ray muttered.

Fran cut her eyes toward him briefly, then focused again on the cut, pulling free the last bit of gravel. "I don't think I'm the one to ask."

In spite of it all, Ray almost grinned. Instead, only the corner of his mouth jerked. "Thanks, Fran."

She paused, watching him for a moment.

"What?"

"Do you think he was shooting at you or June?"

Ray scowled. "Why?"

Fran shrugged one shoulder again. "It's a little unnerving to know someone's out there randomly shooting at folks. I mean, it's easy to assume that it was because of Pastor Gallagher's murder, but was it really?"

Ray's eyes narrowed. "Fran, for all our sakes, let's

hope it's connected. I'd hate to think we've got *two* nut-cases running around in Bell County."

Fran stood. "You're going to need four or five stitches in this arm, so sit tight. Dr. Collins will be over here in a few. Do *not* go wandering around looking for June. Even if she is nearby." She winked at him, then left the room.

Ray twisted his forearm, tipping the gauze onto the tray where his arm rested. His muscles still twitched from the pain. Much of the blood had clotted, but a few places still glistened red from the cleansing of it. It was only three inches long, but deep in the center. Scrapes surrounded the primary wound, and a bruise had started to form.

Ray looked up at the room. How he hated being in the hospital. It reminded him of pain and loss—nothing good, that was for sure. The last time he'd been stuck in the hospital was with Anne, when she was dying of cancer. He'd done everything he could since his wife's death to avoid the place. But now it was June who brought him here—how strange.

He stretched his fingers out, then made a fist, grateful that the tendons remained unscathed. He repeated the action, imagining his grip closing on the man who'd shot at June....

"Don't you dare undo all my work." Fran's scolding drowned out the greeting of Dr. Collins, who followed the nurse into the room.

Ray focused on the doctor, whose busy night in the

E.R. showed in the shadows around his eyes. "How's June?"

Nick Collins plucked a pair of latex gloves out of a box on the wall and stretched them over his hands. "Obstinate. She's not thrilled about being kept overnight."

"You're keeping her for observation only?"

Nick nodded, then peered over his glasses at the tray Fran had prepped. "They're moving her to her room. Go see her when we're done here. Hopefully, you can save the second-shift nurses some grief."

June's head throbbed, and every time she moved it, a new wave of vertigo slammed into her, making the room spin.

"You missed lunch, but I can order you a tray for later. What would you like for supper?" the nurse's aide asked.

June closed her eyes and pressed her head against the pillow, hoping it would stop. "A bucket."

In the silence that followed, she relented, opened her eyes and squinted at the aide, who waited next to her bed. "I'm too dizzy to eat. Don't order anything."

"The meds will take care of the dizziness. You'll be hungry later."

"I'll order out for pizza." She closed her eyes again and scratched idly at the heart-monitor patch peeking out of the top of her gown. Near the head of the bed, the monitor blinked, its bright green sinus-rhythm line showing steady and even. "Please go away."

"I'll be back later." The aide's shoes squeaked lightly on the floor as she turned and left the room.

Before the door could shut, however, someone caught it and entered the room. June started to repeat her command to go away when she realized that her new visitor had arrived with the scent of sweat, musk, dirt, gunfire residue and the faint odor of cologne that somehow still lingered after the day's events.

"Hi, Ray."

"You had to get hurt, didn't you?"

"I guess it does sort of put a damper on the possibility of me as suspect." She opened her eyes and peered at him through the pain.

"More or less." He stepped closer to the bed. "How do you feel?"

"Like a major-league baseball after the World Series."

"Mets or Yankees?"

She grinned, which made her wince. "Red Sox. Don't make me laugh."

Ray returned the smile, then reached for her hand. "I'm sorry."

"Oh? You put the sniper on that hill?"

"I dropped my guard. Our cruisers don't just suddenly have flats."

She glowered at him. "Sniper. Lying in wait. Nothing you could have done."

"I could have called—"

June clutched his hand. "Stop it, Ray. You start getting all overprotective on me and we'll never solve David's murder."

Ray's eyes narrowed. *"We."*

"I've been thinking about something—"

"You've been smacked in the head."

"Doesn't stop me from thinking."

He pointed at the badge on his chest, then at her. "Me, sheriff. You, witness. Solving this is my job, not yours."

"Don't worry, Tarzan, I'll let you be the hero." June tugged on his hand to pull him closer. "But there are some things you don't know."

Ray listened silently as June spoke. He knew that her mind never stopped, that she always had some project, some plan in the works, whether it was remodeling a Victorian parsonage or a craft session for the kinder-garteners at the church. Apparently, her brain had been spinning about David's murder from the moment she'd found the body. Her ideas were astute and in many ways mirrored his own thinking about the murder.

She felt it wasn't random, but local, intentional and related to David's newfound political ambition. As far as she knew, nothing else had changed in his life. And she also felt that she had not interrupted the murder itself—but possibly the reason for it.

"If you had interrupted the murder," Ray said, "there would have been less blood and probably no footprints. Whoever bolted out that door did it without caring that he'd stepped in the blood."

"I barged in because I saw the footprints on the porch. And someone was still there."

"Ransacking the study."

She nodded, then pressed her palm to her forehead. Ray could see that pain still raged inside her. She took a deep breath, wiped her face with one hand and sat straighter in the bed. *She won't give up. Or give in.*

"I must have interrupted the search in David's study."

Ray pulled a chair next to the bed and sat. "The way they left, as well as the evidence, definitely points to a division in the team. Whoever went out the back ran first or you would have run into him. Probably the mastermind was more afraid of getting caught. The person who left out the back may have been the killer since there was blood evidence in the tunnel. He left last, more determined to finish the job."

"He was just the muscle."

Ray's mouth twitched at June's use of the term, and he shifted in the chair. "And not as concerned about you catching him. He may have planned on killing you, then heard us in the driveway."

June's eyes watered again, and she looked down, plucking at the blanket across her lap. "David once told me he could hear the Corvette turn into the driveway. Teased me that it gave him plenty of time to escape out the back."

Ray gave her a moment of memory. "Is that why you went to the back door?"

Her gentle smile revealed her deep affection for David

Gallagher. "Yes. After he said that, I always went to the back. It made him laugh."

"Didn't most people go to the back?"

June's hands stilled and her brow furrowed. "No." She looked up at Ray, a light of realization in her eyes. "No, they didn't. When JR and I first remodeled, people got in the habit of coming to the back, but JR didn't like it. He wanted to be accessible to everyone but not encourage folks to think they could just walk in any time. At that time, the driveway came around behind the house, so he solved the issue by putting in the patio there at the side of the house and improving the sidewalk in the front. Even though the driveway still went around it to our garage, people started coming up the front walk."

"So instead of building a physical barrier or offending people by asking them not to come to the back, he built a psychological barrier."

"And most people got the message." June pushed herself up in the bed. "And David carried that tradition forward after JR died. The only people who came to the back were people he knew extremely well. He'd never have opened the back door to a stranger. And he was austere enough in the pulpit that casual acquaintances never even thought about it. Except for his political cronies, you'll have to look at his friends."

"Our friends."

They both fell silent, well aware of how small the Bell County community was. The population of the three small towns of the county—White Hills, Caralinda and the county seat of Bell Springs—remained tiny enough that most people knew everyone in the area. That was one reason that June remained a respected voice in Bell County.

Ray cleared his throat. "You were David's psychological barrier."

June scowled. "What?"

"The reason he wanted you on Hunter's side. Like it or not, people still listen to you in Bell County. If you come out in a vocal way against Hunter, he'll have a hard time advancing politically."

"Ray, I think you're giving me too much credit."

Ray shook his head. "No, I'm not. Do you still blog every day?"

June hesitated a moment, then nodded. June's online diary had begun almost as self-therapy after JR's death. Titled "June's Bell County Wanderings," she had started it in an effort to connect with other pastors' widows. Granted, at thirty, she was younger than most of them. But sharing her grief, however, had soon turned into sharing her life in Bell County, and the popularity of the blog had soared. She entertained people with tales of life in a small Southern town, and she now had more than one thousand followers, most of them in the county.

"I'm fairly sure David wouldn't want you talking about Hunter's exploits online."

"Ray Taylor, I do not gossip, thank you very much. I do not—"

Ray took her hand. "I know that. But if you had supported Hunter openly…"

She hesitated, looking down at their intertwined fingers. "People might listen. Might."

"Right."

"Which explains David's actions toward me, but—" She paused and her eyes widened. "You think Hunter will ask me to support him?"

Ray squeezed her hand. "Hard to say. But if he does approach you, you may be able to expand on any information we get from him."

June took a deep breath. "How? Do you think Hunter would tell me if he knew what the killer was after?"

Ray watched June's face closely. "What do *you* think he was after?"

"You're asking what a pastor keeps in his study?" She shrugged. "Depends a lot on the pastor. And the church. Gospel Immanuel is small enough that JR did most of his work at home."

"So he kept anything valuable in his study?"

"And anything private."

"What kind of private information did JR have?"

"Counseling. He helped a lot of people, and he was a fanatic about people's privacy. Any notes he kept from counseling sessions were locked away in a fireproof box and stored in one of the dozens of hiding places in the house. He didn't even tell *me* where they were."

Ray shifted, then stood, reluctantly letting go of June's hand. Counseling records could provide a motivation for murder. *David, what in the world did you get into? What got you killed?* "Did JR tell David?"

She shrugged. "No way of knowing now." She

plucked at the sheet again. "I don't know if David took on any of JR's folks for counseling. That's not the kind of information anyone shares."

Ray nodded. "There were a lot of hiding places in the house?"

"It's an old Victorian, and the original owner, Sieg-fried Osborne, was a little nutty. Siegfried, as you know, was the grandfather of Rosalie Osborne. Poor thing just vanished into thin air. Her disappearance was never solved, right?"

Ray shook his head. "And we've got enough to worry about without adding anyone else to the mix, June."

June gave Ray a small smile. "Anyway, we uncovered at least a hundred secret cubbyholes, rooms and sliding panels. Every time we moved a wall or redid paneling, we found something."

Ray stared. "You found stuff?"

"Oh, yeah. That house is a time capsule. Letters, diaries, dried flowers. Jewelry, silver, candlesticks. JR once found a tin box full of papers that…" As her voice trailed off, June grew still and the color left her face.

"What was in the box?"

"I don't really know. He wouldn't let me see it. We'd discussed everything else, but he wouldn't let me see that one box. He said he planned to destroy it, the box and all the contents."

"Why?"

"I don't know." June clutched Ray's hand again. "He

just promised to get rid of it, said what was inside was far too dangerous to keep in the house."

Ray closed both hands around hers as they turned to ice in his grasp. "Looks like he may have been right."

FIVE

"How did he know where we were headed?"

Daniel grimaced and squirmed a bit in the visitor's chair of Ray's office. The late-afternoon sun always shone directly through the windows and Daniel shifted the chair so that the blinds shaded his face. "Maybe he has a scanner. We did notify dispatch that you were taking June to NorthCrest."

Ray stared at his deputy. "Maybe."

"You don't buy it."

"You radioed after we pulled out of the driveway."

"Right, so I could give them a reasonable ETA."

"The attack happened about ten minutes later."

Daniel thought for a moment, then dipped one shoulder in acquiescence. "Not enough time for him to find a place and get set up. He had to know sooner."

"How?" Ray waited, still and outwardly calm. He knew his ability to remain motionless unnerved some people, even a couple of his own officers. Daniel wasn't one of them. Also former military, Daniel shared the ability to watch and wait.

In addition to knowing that, unlike the other officers, Ray would be headed for NorthCrest, the shooter would have had to know—or be told—the best route from the parsonage to the hospital. He'd have to know the area, know what would be the best location for a good shot. He would have to get there, get set up. And he'd have to know which cruiser Ray drove.

Daniel leaned forward. "If he shot at you in the tunnel, maybe he just figured you might go to the hospital."

"But he wouldn't know that I'd have June with me."

"You think this is about June."

"I think it's about David Gallagher. June just got caught in the middle. But the shots in the tunnel weren't about me."

"They were about the shirt. But he did see you."

"I didn't see him."

"Would he know that for sure?"

"With that spot in my eyes, yes."

"But they had to know June didn't see them, either."

Ray leaned back in his chair, his arms resting on the edge of his desk. "I don't think they're worried about June seeing them. I suspect they think she knows why David was killed."

"Does she?"

Ray hesitated. His conversation with June at the hospital had raised more questions than it had answered, including what she might know about the contents of David's study. "I don't know. The problem is, I don't think she knows, either." Ray took a deep breath. "Okay,

I want you to alert the local body shops about SUV repairs, and check the usual illegal dump sites for fresh tracks or signs of recent activity."

"Right. The lake cliffs, the quarry, Sanderson's ravine."

Ray nodded. "Who's at the parsonage?"

"Brent Carter. Gage took the evidence to the lab."

"Good. June interrupted the search," Ray said, "so whatever they were after is still there. I want two officers on the house today, and I want you and Carter there tonight. Search it again from top to bottom. And make sure no one gets in that house, or even near it. I'll get June over there tomorrow. I hate to ask for the double shift, but—"

"It's needed. I'll be there."

"If you find that SUV, call me."

Daniel's eyebrows bunched together. "You're involving June in the search?"

Ray let out a long sigh. "Not my preferred choice, but she told me that the house is riddled with secret hiding places. She and JR found a lot of them, but she thinks there are more. My guess is that if David concealed something that got him killed, it's in one of those hiding places."

"You think they'll try to search the house again?"

"I know they will. I want the officers at the house in vests. I don't think these people care who they have to kill. I want a cruiser in front of the house and a cruiser in the rear, and I want that tunnel sealed. I want reports every thirty minutes. And I want a man on June's home."

Daniel's scowl deepened. "You don't think they'll stop with another attempt on the parsonage?"

Ray shook his head. "Someone hired a killer with combat training to set this in motion. It's a long way from over."

Lord, I had forgotten how much I hate hospitals. Help me be nice to these— "Ouch!"

"Sorry."

June inhaled deeply and swallowed a growl. "Does this mean I'm going home?"

The young nurse continued her efforts to remove the tape securing June's IV to her arm. "I suspect so. The doctor ordered this removed. Okay, I'm going to pull it out. It might sting just a bit." Pressing two fingers over the insertion point, she slid the IV out with the other hand. "Press here."

June used her own fingers to replace the nurse's and pressed on the vein until the nurse could apply the bandage. "How long do I leave this on?"

"You can take it off this afternoon. But no heavy lifting for a couple of days."

June swung her legs over the edge of the bed and stood up. "Honey, I avoid heavy lifting most days."

The nurse grinned. "Well, if I had Sheriff Taylor waiting on me hand and foot, I would, too."

June froze, staring at the young girl. "Ray's not—"

"He's in the hallway, to take you home."

"I called someone—"

"You might want to call them back. The sheriff doesn't look much in the mood to take no for an answer."

June remained still a moment longer, then stiffened her spine and took a deep breath. *Right. If this is what he thinks needs to be done...* "Could you please ask Sheriff Taylor to give me a few moments? I need to get dressed and make that call."

"Of course. I'll ask him to wait until the charge nurse brings your paperwork."

"Thank you."

June watched the girl leave, then sank back down on the bed, her heart in her throat. Of course he'd want to talk to her again. Yesterday, she'd virtually shoved her way into his investigation. And then she'd remembered that box.

June looked down at her hands, opening and closing them as if they suddenly felt empty. She had a sudden urge to clasp Ray's hands again, feel the strength of them closing around hers....

June shook her hands furiously, then scrubbed her face with her palms, trying to brush away the feelings that flooded over her. *Friend. Repeat. He's a friend.* She took two deep breaths this time, letting each out slowly. *Focus on David. On how you can help. On what you know about the house.*

June looked down at her hands again, where her wedding rings still glistened. Three years later, she still wore them, a symbol of the many ways she'd never let go of Jackie Rhea Eaton.

"I still go to your church." Her whispered words sounded flat. "Still embrace your friends. And all the things you'd taught me."

Jackie Rhea's wife. It had been her identity for most of her adult life. He'd taken her off the streets. Turned her from a street kid into the preacher's wife. If she let go of him, then she let go of the very identity that kept her from going back, from being…

Nothing.

June shivered, an old, familiar rush of fear chilling her spine. A fear she'd fought since the day JR died. She'd been forced from the house they'd renovated and made their own, but she'd held on to everything else. She liked Ray, admired him. But she couldn't…

Stop dwelling on foolishness! Get dressed! June stood and pulled on the clothes that her sister April had brought last night. She slipped into the jeans and red blouse, then reached for the makeup bag.

June grinned as she unzipped the bag and pulled out the hairbrush, toothbrush and foundation. "Bless you, sweetie. You knew."

Yep, April knew that June would never want to leave the hospital without putting on the face of the preacher's wife. In the past twenty-four hours she'd found David dead, been shot at and tumbled down a ravine, but some things did not change.

No matter how nice it felt to hold Ray's hand, she was still JR's wife.

* * *

Ray Taylor stood outside June's hospital room with his thoughts swirling in a maelstrom, ranging from irritation at June's delay to rage at yesterday's events. The idea that someone in Bell County would have such dire secrets that he'd be willing to hire an assassin to protect them was both outrageous and ludicrous. And how was it possible that he, as sheriff, would be so unaware of such hidden dangers?

Bell County remained small, in size, population and, for the most part, way of life. People lived here precisely because they wanted a simpler, quieter existence. Sure Bell County had its share of crime, but it remained manageable. Plus, his officers blanketed the county, living in the towns they patrolled. He had informants in every drug ring and gambling operation in the area. Twice he'd arrested human traffickers at the truck stop out at the interstate, and the owners there knew better than to let girls try to—

What is taking her so long?

Ray glanced at the door to June's room again. The nurse had gone in with the discharge papers a few moments ago, and Ray realized that he'd grown increasingly impatient with the delay in starting both his day and his investigation.

Since when are you impatient about anything?

Since this murder expanded beyond Bell County.

Ray's thoughts spun to a standstill. He'd discussed with Daniel the likelihood that David's murder wasn't random, and they had focused on it being local because of the evidence. Obviously, the killers had known David as well as the local area.

But Ray had awakened this morning with a nagging mental itch at the back of his mind, and it had grown stronger throughout the past couple of hours. A hunch, and over the years in law enforcement, Ray had learned to trust his hunches. He pulled out his cell phone.

"Have you pulled David's financial records yet?" he asked.

"Gage is working on that," Daniel replied.

"In addition to checking for suspicious activity, make sure you check for any unusual banking locations."

"You mean like out-of-town ATMs?"

"Anything that raises an eyebrow. Strange ATMs, foreign banks."

Daniel got the hint. "You mean offshore."

"Anything."

"You think he was being bribed? Or was doing the bribing?"

"Don't want to assume anything yet. And remember, he's a respected pastor. Tread carefully."

"Gotcha. I'll keep you posted."

"You been to sleep yet?"

Daniel hesitated. "Gage and I decided to check a few more things. The parsonage was quiet last night, but we're still wired."

"Unwire and go to bed. It'll take awhile for the bank records to be pulled. I need you both alert if this picks up speed suddenly."

"Will do."

Ray closed his phone and pocketed it again, just as the nurse emerged from June's room. "You can go in now."

"Thank you."

Ray pushed open the door and stopped. Yesterday he'd seen June at her worst—distraught, covered in blood, bruised and unconscious. The last time he'd seen her in this room, a bandage covered the left side of her face and an IV had tethered her to the bed. An injured woman, the victim of violence.

The June in front of him now was no victim. Even wearing the simple outfit of jeans and a red shirt, June had transformed back into the strong woman he'd been admiring for quite some time. Hair brushed, makeup pristine, the white gauze replaced with two tiny butterfly bandages, she was placing her makeup kit and brush back into the bag April had brought for her. She smiled at him, and for a moment Ray's chest tightened.

Yesterday, he'd desperately wanted to protect her. Today, he was reminded of how magnificent June truly was.

"I see you've bounced back from the edge."

June's smile widened. "Amazing what a little sleep and a lot of makeup will do." She lifted the bag. "April could have picked me up."

Ray shook his head. "I'm afraid you're going to remain with me until this is settled."

June grew still and her smile faded. "You're not serious."

"Quite serious. That shooter meant to kill you, not

me. I'm convinced they believe you saw them, or you know something. Either way, you are apparently a liability. You're in their way."

June's gaze grew distant, as if the words had triggered a painful memory.

"June?"

Before she could answer, Ray's cell phone rang, and he pulled it from his pocket. "Taylor."

Daniel's voice on the other end was tight. "Ray, you better get over to the parsonage now."

"What's happened?"

Daniel cleared his throat again, and Ray knew it had to be bad if his chief deputy was fighting to hold it together. "In yesterday's turmoil, we left June's car at the parsonage. Gage went out there a few minutes ago, planning to drop it back at June's house on his way home. He started it, then left it running to warm up, like June said. Brent called him back into the parsonage to ask him something. Good thing."

A sudden chill clenched Ray's spine. "What happened?"

"It blew up."

SIX

"JR gave me that car." June stared at the smoldering hunks of metal and leather that had once been a 1968 emerald-green Corvette convertible, her eyes glazed, her body numb. "Our second anniversary. He knew I liked the green-and-tan combination, the Roadster. I loved that car. But it was a mess. JR tinkered with it almost every Saturday the first year we had it, just to keep it running." June's monotone monologue trailed off. The true impact of the car's destruction began seeping into her entire body, chilling her. She shivered and crossed her arms.

"I'm sorry." Ray's voice, low and rumbling close behind her, held sincere regret.

"This is why you didn't want me out of your sight."

"Yes."

"That was meant for me."

"No doubt."

She glanced from the car to Ray's deputy. Jeff Gage looked a tad shaken, but he moved around the crime scene smoothly, helping the fire chief examine evidence. "But Jeff is okay."

"Thank God."

June hugged herself a bit tighter, fighting the surge of swirling emotions that boiled within her. She wanted to scream at everything that had happened over the past twenty-four hours. But that would do no good. It was one of the things JR had impressed on her. *I can't control the way I feel, but I can control the way I act.* June took a deep breath and looked at the Corvette's remains again.

"Y'know, JR actually hated that car."

"He told me once." Ray shifted his weight. "He didn't think you knew."

June smiled wryly. "JR tried hard to keep it a secret. But a wife knows her husband." She paused a moment. "I only wish…"

"What?"

She motioned toward the ruin. "I only wish I hadn't left my purse in the trunk yesterday."

Ray made an odd coughing noise, and she twisted to look at him, just in time to see him swallow a grin and force a solemn look back on his face.

She smacked his arm. "Hey, it's not funny. My cell phone was in there. And my cards and license. You going to drive me around until I get them replaced?"

He tilted his head and smiled at her. "That was pretty much my plan anyway."

"Sheriff?"

They both turned toward a young man, swathed in

firefighting gear, who held out a small, burnt box that looked like a cross between a 9-volt battery and an alarm clock.

"What's that?" Ray asked.

"It used to be a timed detonator switch." Michael Dearborn, formerly a demolitions expert for the army, was the only member of the White Hills Fire Department with any experience in explosives. He turned the device over a couple of times, then held it gingerly in one palm. "Gage told me he'd been in the house a few minutes before the car went up. Not sure why they set it for a delay like that."

Ray crossed his arms. "Because that car had to warm up before it would go into gear."

Michael's eyes narrowed. "Say again?"

June squeezed her eyes shut. "I *really* don't want to hear this," she said aloud, her voice a bare whisper.

Ray placed a hand on her shoulder, its weight a warm comfort that startled June somewhat. "June's car is—"

"Was. As in *used* to be. Not anymore."

The hand on her shoulder tightened a bit as he went on. "*Was* unusual. It needed to warm up about ten minutes before the transmission could be shifted. June's habit was to start the car, then go back into the house. But my guess is they didn't know that. Whoever set this wanted the car well away from the parsonage before it blew, so the explosion wouldn't take out the house with the Corvette." Ray motioned to the scorched walls and two shattered windows. "Whatever they need is still in that house."

Michael let out a long, weary breath and closed his hand around the device. "We just happened to be close when the call came in. Otherwise, the house would have been gone."

June, who had barely glanced at the damage to the parsonage, now ached as much for her former home as for her car. Her throat tightened, as if something crucial were slipping away from her, slowly but inevitably.

"...attempted homicide." Ray finished a sentence June had not heard.

Michael nodded. "We don't know what the explosive was yet, but this is definitely not an accident."

"Probably something thrown together in a hurry, not as well planned as the murder. I doubt they had June in mind when they killed David. We had cars front and back last night to cover the entrances, but nothing here at the side of the house."

"I'll see what additional evidence we can find when it cools off some."

June approached the ruins of the car slowly, her thoughts blurred and scattered. This was JR's beautiful gift to her, gone forever. The top, leather seats and tires had burned away. The frame sat flat on the ground, only the barest components of what had once been an amazing vehicle remaining, steaming from the heat and water. The blast shattered the motor, and debris spread over the driveway, patio and yard. Two pieces had been embedded in the side of the house.

Yet she didn't feel the loss as intensely as she'd expected to when Ray first broke the news to her at the hospital. She'd felt dizzy with shock at first, but now she just felt—what?

June glanced at where the trunk had been. The concern that buzzed in her brain still focused on her purse, not the car itself. And the house. Her eyes narrowed as the smoke from the rubble stung her eyes. But what was this other feeling?

Relief?

The firefighters buzzed around her, gathering their gear and preparing to leave. At the edge of the yard, the crowd had gathered again, whispering. June ignored them. She didn't care what they had to say.

She had lost the last of JR, the last remaining piece of his memory, which she had clung to with all her might. She wanted to hurt for him, for this precious reminder of him. Yet the emotion that captured her was not grief. She moved closer, searching her mind and heart for a sense of anger, of loss. But the image that flashed through her brain was of Ray.

Ray, his injuries covered with tape and gauze.

He saved my life.

The thought made June swallow hard. In pushing her out of the cruiser and making sure she was out of the line of fire, in sending the sniper scurrying for cover, Ray Taylor had saved her life.

Ray, who was injured because of her.

Dear Lord, what have I done?

Focused on her thoughts, June didn't see the lump of charred metal in front of her until she tripped, and one foot came down on the debris, slipping wildly. She stumbled hard, crying out, her arms lashing out in front of her to brace her fall.

An arm locked around her waist like a vise, and she swung to her right, firmly braced against Ray. His other hand caught her left arm, settling her on her feet again. His concerned expression reflected his gentle words. "Careful. You're stepping on my evidence."

Ray had been right behind her the entire time, not letting her stray too far away. He had not left her. "Thank you. I'll watch where I'm going."

He released her and stepped back. "Why don't you wait in the house? I'll be in shortly."

"Good idea." June turned and headed for the back door. She climbed the steps slowly, avoiding the now brown, shoe-shaped stains on the porch. The screen door creaked as she opened it, a noise she had not noticed yesterday. She paused, peering at the hinges.

As she stood there, staring at the door frame, other images of recent visits to the house flashed through June's mind, winking like fireflies on a hot, dark night. Peeling wallpaper in a bathroom. Darkened light bulbs. A water stain on a ceiling. Nothing major, just small signs of a home being ignored.

What else did you neglect, David?

June felt a twinge of guilt for thinking ill of the dead, and she shuddered as she looked around the kitchen, its contents still in disarray and the sticky pool of blood remaining as a stark reminder of yesterday's violence. A faint smell of decay lingered in the air, and a couple of flies buzzed, disturbed by June's appearance in the room.

Her gaze searched the kitchen, looking for other signs that David's life had been out of order. A Victorian like this one required a lot of maintenance, and over the past few months, David had not taken care of the parsonage, nor asked the church's board for help.

Since, technically, the house belonged to the church, the board could have stepped in to protect and maintain the property, but the entire congregation at White Hills Gospel Immanuel had respected David Gallagher's privacy. He had not asked for help, so none had been offered. Now shingles dropped to the ground during the spring rains, and the gutters overflowed. The house had not been painted, and the lattice work on the porch bowed under the weight of overgrown vines.

Looking around the kitchen, June could spot a dozen small things that could have been taken care of easily. A drippy faucet. A cracked tile. A dead plant. June's brows came together. "What were you doing with your time, David?"

"Say again?"

June swung around. Ray stood on the porch, watching her through the screen door.

"Why were you asking about his time?"

June opened her arms wide to indicate the kitchen and beyond. "When JR and I lived here, this house was pristine. David always said he admired that. When he moved in, he promised me he'd honor the work JR and I had done on the house."

"And?"

"And for the first two years or so, he did a decent job with the small things. Then about eight months ago, everything started falling apart."

"You're sure of the time frame?"

June stood straighter. "Believe me. I did not want to leave this house. I loved it here. I've watched every chip of paint, every stray weed, every loose nail since I left it."

Ray opened the screen door and stepped inside.

Pointing at the door, June said, "See? He didn't even bother to oil the hinges. I've been in and out of this house for dinners and meetings, and every time I've seen something else that needs repair. He once told me the third-floor toilet didn't work anymore, but since he didn't use it, he didn't bother fixing it."

"So you're upset about the house?"

"I'm upset because I nagged him about the house without realizing it meant something other than him being neglectful. That it meant David had other fish to fry."

"So you think that whatever this is all about, it dates back eight months or so."

She nodded. "At least." She inhaled deeply. "Look, a pastor's time is tight. People think they just go on visits and write sermons, but there's a lot more to being a good senior pastor. There's a great deal of administrative work to do. That's why JR went off for two weeks every year to plan his sermons, and why he asked the church to bring David on as the associate."

Ray remained still. "But David never brought on anyone to help."

"Just the secretaries. And they're part-time. That's not enough for a church this size. He should have requested the board put together a search committee for a new associate within a few months of taking over. But he didn't."

"Couldn't that explain the house neglect? Too much work?"

"It could, but why *didn't* he bring on help, if he was struggling with the house and the church? And why did he do fine with the house for more than two years, then let everything go at once? It would have been incredibly easy for him to just ask the board to help find an associate or even a handyman. Instead, he kept to himself. What if he didn't bring on help because he was hiding something?"

Ray stepped closer to her. "What do you think he was hiding?"

"I thought figuring out stuff like that was your job."

Ray's fleeting smile disappeared quickly. "So it is. I usually start with evidence."

"David's study."

"You lead the way."

June headed out of the kitchen, Ray following, eyes alert. Part of him felt he should get her out of here so she could rest, but he knew she would have none of it. June paused only briefly as they passed through a butler's pantry, waving at one of the walls. "We found two hidden compartments in the pantry, but JR took down the paneling that hid them and turned them into a computer center. We had a laptop stationed there that kept track of all the church and parsonage events, as well as the general needs of the house. Kitty Parker, JR's assistant, did a lot of the updates."

"I remember Kitty. Did she have a key to the house?"

June took a right down a short hallway leading to the pastor's study and a guest bedroom. "Sure. She was David's assistant until a few months ago when she married. She married one of Daniel's cousins, a mechanic I think, and they live up in Franklin, just over the state line."

Ray pulled a small notebook out of his pocket and wrote down Kitty's name. "Was marriage the only reason she left?"

June glowered over her shoulder at him. "David was a gentleman."

Ray's mouth tightened. "I never implied otherwise. But you obviously know where all the secrets are hidden in this church, if not the county."

June opened to door of the study. "A lot of them. But not all. And the ones I know, I don't talk about."

"Kitty and her husband are no longer members here?"

June nodded. "He already had a church home in Kentucky when they met. Wanted to go where his mama did— Oh, wow."

They both stopped and looked around at the wild disarray of David Gallagher's study. The room, large enough for an expansive cherry desk, visitor chairs and a seating area made up of a couch and a wingback, lay in shambles. Bookcases lined two walls, and many of the books had been pulled out and tossed about the room. The desk had been thoroughly ransacked, with the files, office supplies and personal items yanked out and flung with fury. The top of the desk had been swept clean, and a once-elegant pen set lay smashed and crushed on the floor.

Signs of June's interruption of the search also stood out clearly as the tall windows behind the desk bathed the room in dust-filled rays of the morning sun. The cherry credenza sat along one wall, parallel to the desk, and while the four file drawers underneath its polished top had been pulled open, the contents remained untouched.

Ray moved slowly past June and squatted next to the damaged desk set, barely aware that June had silently followed, standing behind him.

"What is it?" she asked softly.

"We processed this room yesterday. Took the pictures. Checked for prints."

"And?"

"I didn't notice that this had not just been broken. It's been stomped."

"Emotional."

"Especially when you're in a hurry and the owner is already dead. It's a wasted moment."

"Not just anger. Vengeful rage."

"So what would a pastor do that would make someone this angry?"

"Not a pastor."

June's words were so firm and even that Ray stood, turning his attention to her. "How do you mean that?"

She shook her head slowly. "If something he did made someone this angry, he probably did it as a man outside his profession."

"Maybe this anger isn't really aimed at David. Maybe it's at whatever the killer was looking for in this house and David just got in the way."

June's chin came up, and her eyes brightened. "David wouldn't have kept it in here. This is where he counseled people. It would be too public a place to keep something dangerous enough to get him killed."

"Did you and JR tell him about the compartments?"

"JR did once, when they were talking about having enough storage in the house."

"Then let's start with the ones you found. See what turns up."

June spun and headed for the bookcase near the door. "Then we'll have to be methodical about it, or we'll miss one. There are two in here. But most are on the second and third floors, with a few in the attic."

"What about the tunnel?"

She pointed at him. "Good thought. I know there's one on the wall with the ladder."

Ray scowled, thinking of the narrow descent into the earth beneath the house. "Seriously?"

June headed for one of the bookcases, where she cleared the remaining books from a shelf and pushed aside a narrow panel at the back. "You wouldn't believe where some of these things are hidden. After finding fifteen or twenty, JR decided it had been a game to Siegfried Osborne."

Ray followed her to what appeared to be a decorative series of beveled insets in the wall behind the desk. June pressed on the edge of one of the bevels near the floor. A door swung open, and she peered up at him. "Flashlight?"

Ray removed a small but powerful flashlight from his belt and handed it to her. She took it and swung the beam around inside a niche about the size of a small wall safe. Empty.

She snapped off the light and straightened. "Once we found a bundle of Osborne's letters. He obsessed over the tiniest things. Paranoid. He saw evil around every corner. Heard voices in the walls and worried about having his ideas copied. He wrote every letter twice, mailing one and keeping a copy. But he was brilliant. He corresponded with architects, artists, writers, politicians, all kinds of people. In one of the letters, he gloated that his wife still had not discovered all his 'squirrel nests.' In another, he mentioned that he and the architect for the house had designed more than fifty of them, but there were more than that."

"And how many did you and JR find?"

"Around a hundred."

Ray touched her arm as she closed the panel. "There are more still hidden?"

She nodded. "I'm sure of it." June froze a second, then her eyes widened. "We kept a list on the kitchen computer, and JR suggested David add to it if he found more." Ducking around him, June headed back to the converted butler's pantry. She opened the curtain to let in more light, then pushed the window up.

"A little fresh air won't hurt. I can't believe it still smells so strongly in here."

Ray's brows furrowed. "It is strong, but not unusual for a crime scene."

June pulled forward a laptop that had been tucked into a shelf and checked to see if it was still plugged in. "Your men must have overlooked this since it was back in its niche."

Ray stood behind her as she booted up the laptop. "Wouldn't he have changed the password?"

"We'll find out." Silently, they waited as the screen flipped through the start-up process and the dialog box for the password popped up. Carefully, she tapped in the word *Immanuel*.

It worked, and June bounced up on her toes. "Yes! We're in." Deftly, she maneuvered the mouse around, searching through the folders until she found one labeled "Squirrels." She opened the folder, which contained several nonsequential numbered documents, as well as one labeled "Squirrel Niches." She clicked on it.

"So I guess you started the list."

June looked over her shoulder at him. "What?"

"The file name. Fits you more than JR."

June paused, her eyes searching his face. "Really?"

Ray realized abruptly how much he loved the blue in her eyes when she looked up at him like this, and he took a small step backward, shifting his weight to his left foot. "Really."

June grinned. "Yeah. I started it. Seemed appropriate. We numbered them as we found them. The numbered documents are a list of contents that we found. That's why the numbers seem random. Not every niche held something. In fact, a lot were empty."

He pointed at the computer. "Did David add to the main list?"

She refocused, scrolling down the page. "Yes. Right here, these last five entries are new. I'll print it off so we will know we've hit them all." The printer began scratching out the page. The paper had just landed in the tray when they heard a hollow popping sound from outside the house. The computer beeped suddenly and the screen went dark.

June stared at it. "What in the world—?"

A slice of cold apprehension slid up Ray's spine. "We've lost power."

"But why would—?"

June's words ended in a scream as the window of the pantry splintered with an explosive crack and the computer screen disintegrated in a shower of sparks.

SEVEN

Ray flung his arms around June, his body twisting away from the window, swinging both of them to the floor. Above their heads, the computer and its shelf splintered wildly, showering them with bits of plastic and wood. June's scream echoed off the walls, ending suddenly as Ray clamped a hand over her mouth.

June shuddered, fighting the urge to claw his hand away. Panic sliced through her, and every instinct, every muscle, wanted to fight. As if he knew, Ray tightened his arms around her, his voice low and remarkably calm in her ear.

"June, be still. Listen. Listen, sweetheart, just listen."

He pressed his weight over her, forcing her muscles to relax. The low, repeated words had the intended effect, as her panic-driven tremors eased. "The officers outside are responding. You're safe. I'll keep you safe."

June closed her eyes.

Ray's voice, almost like a lullaby, continued in her ears. June listened. Shouts from the officers and firefighters still on the scene echoed off the walls of the house. She heard the growl of tires on gravel, the roar of the high-powered engines, the screams of sirens.

The rush of terror, the gripping panic that had sheared through her, slid away slowly as a sliver of scripture echoed in her mind, a reflection of Ray's murmured words.

Be not afraid. In response, a fervent prayer burst through June's mind. *Lord, help me be not afraid. Guide me…us…through this.*

June took a deep breath and let it out slowly, a gentle peace replacing the fear. As it did, Ray's grip on her eased, as if he knew. She opened her eyes as he moved away and stood, then took his offered hand, letting him pull her to her feet.

Ray brushed a strand of hair away from her face. "You okay?"

She nodded, searching his face. The concern in his eyes deepened, and his fingers lingered on a lock of her hair. June's breath caught in her throat, a sudden awareness of the depth of his affection sweeping over her.

"Ray! June!" Daniel's deep bellow jarred them both, and Ray stepped back, his expression shifting to that of a county sheriff on the job, jaw firm, eyes critical and examining.

June turned away, looking at the remnants of the computer as Daniel skidded into the pantry. She plucked at random pieces that lay spread over the inset workstation.

"Are y'all hurt?"

"We're fine. Anyone injured out there?"

June listened, her thoughts lingering on the work that had been done on this laptop in the years since JR had installed it. Church records. Sunday-school class projects. Household budgets and inventories.

Inventories!

"No, the shots were all aimed at the house. The first one took out the electric meter and the power lines."

"Could you tell where the shots were from?"

June pushed aside two sections of the screen, pulling free the printout of the hidden niches. It had survived the attack.

"Yeah, they came from that stand of trees on the other side of the church. Two of the guys headed in that direction, two others headed for the road on the far side, to see if they could cut him off."

June scanned to the bottom, where David had added five newly found niches. When she reached the last entry, her chest tightened and she felt the blood leave her face.

"Good. No more word on this case goes out over the radios. Use your cell phones. Even with dispatch. And now, we need to get June out of here, safely. June?"

June turned to see Daniel and Ray watching her. Ray looked from her face to the paper, then back again. "What is it?"

"The diaries!" Her voice rasped in her throat. "David found Rosalie's diaries!"

* * *

"That's impossible!" Ray refused to believe June's words. "They're a myth!"

"Who's Rosalie?" asked Daniel.

June faced Ray, her expression set. "Why would David lie on a document only he had access to?"

Ray didn't relent in the face of her logic. "He must have been mistaken. Those dairies don't exist. They never did."

"They must or he wouldn't have listed them."

"Who's Rosalie?"

Ray started to respond, but June turned to Daniel, answering his persistent question with a rapid-fire explanation. "Rosalie Osborne, the granddaughter of the original owner of this house."

Daniel, who had been born and raised in Bell County, picked up her meaning quickly. "The one who ran away sometime in the mid-eighties?"

June shook her head and planted her feet firmly, facing the two men. "She disappeared. She did not run away."

Ray growled. "June, stick to the facts. Don't wander off into the rumors and stories high-school kids make up."

Daniel touched June's arm. "Look, this all happened when I was just a baby. Catch me up."

Ray narrowed his eyes in warning, but June pushed her hair away from her face and plunged into the story. "When JR and I renovated the house, the contractors were full of tales about Rosalie, how she called the sheriff's department one night to report that she'd been assaulted. When the officers arrived, the house was standing open, all the lights on, but no Rosalie."

"And no signs of any attack," Ray added.

Daniel's eyes widened. "That's not what the kids spread around when they're telling spooky stories at campouts."

"No doubt."

"Seriously? No foul play?"

"No *signs* of foul play," June said. "Her purse was still in the house, the car still in the garage. Nothing seemed to be missing. Everything was neat, clean and tidy."

"But Rosalie was gone?"

"Poof. She was the last surviving heir, so her estate remains unclaimed. There was no will, and no one to declare her deceased. The house became the property of the state due to the back taxes. It remained abandoned until JR and I convinced the church to buy it for the parsonage. Information about the diaries—"

"*Rumors* about the diaries," Ray interjected.

"—started circulating after Rosalie's best friend told a reporter that Rosalie wrote down everything that happened in her life, even what she had for breakfast. Combined with the stories about this mysterious man she'd been seeing, who only came to her house at night and no one ever saw her with in public—"

"She was having an affair?"

"Daniel, don't give her ammunition for this wild tale."

"—and everyone became convinced she'd been murdered and her body carted off. They believed the diaries would reveal who the man had been."

"Probably some hardworking soul out of Nashville who could only get up here at night. They ran off to get married."

June scowled at him. He crossed his arms and peered down at her.

"Well, the *rumors* I heard were that Rosalie hated being an Osborne and couldn't wait to get away."

Daniel looked confused as he glanced from Ray to June. "So what are the facts in the case?"

June opened her mouth to speak, but Ray counted off the concrete details on one hand. "Only three. The call was made. The house was open and abandoned. Rosalie Osborne has not been seen or heard from since that night. Everything else is conjecture."

"So what about the diaries?"

Ray and June answered, speaking at the same time.

"Hidden!"

"A myth."

"So what exactly did David find?"

Ray and June looked from Daniel to each other, then Ray pointed at the paper in June's hand. "Only one way to solve this. Where are they?"

June checked the list. "Third-floor bathroom. Panel inside the linen closet, right side, eye level." She rolled her shoulders, and Ray saw the weariness in her eyes as she ran her hand through her hair. "No wonder he wouldn't get the toilet fixed. The pipes run behind that side of the closet."

Ray gestured for Daniel to head out the back door. "Rivers, check on what's going on outside. Find out if they've made progress with finding the shooter."

Daniel opened his mouth to respond, then glanced from Ray to June, then back again. Abruptly, he nodded. "Yes, sir." The young man then turned on his heel and left.

June looked up at Ray. "Is this the part where you tell me I have to leave, for my own good?"

"Your last twenty-four hours have been rough. Are you okay?"

He examined her closely. The skin beneath her eyes looked even darker and more drawn than before. She glanced back at the destroyed computer. "Ray, when I was seventeen, my father kicked me out of the house the day my mother died. I was stabbed my first night on the streets, and I spent the day of her funeral in the hospital. I ate out of Dumpsters and soup kitchens. I've been in jail. I've had worse days."

"Yes, but I didn't ask *will* you be okay, I asked if you *are* okay. I think we should get you out of here."

June rested her hand on his arm. "I need to do this. Not just for David. For me. And besides, you need me, Ray Taylor. I can locate these hiding places faster than anyone."

"What do *you* need?"

She squeezed his arm. "Just don't leave me. I'm getting used to you saving my life."

Her grip on his arm felt warm and comforting, as if she were reaching out to him as much as he was toward her. Ray felt something shift deep inside, something he'd been ignoring since she'd insisted they remain only friends.

He straightened his back and nodded. "I never will. I promise."

Her eyes brightened. "Good. So let's head upstairs. Right?"

Ray stepped back, indicating that she should lead the way. The list still clutched in her hand, June headed toward the staircase at the front of the house.

Ray followed June up the main stairs to the third floor. She paused on the landing, pointing out the suddenly narrowed steps that headed up one more story.

"The third floor was intended as the quarters for the main servants of the first household. Temporary or seasonal employees lived up there, on the top floor, the attic. Hot in summer and frigid in winter. We didn't find as many niches on this floor and in the attic because 'servants couldn't really be trusted with valuables and the attic's climate was too caustic.'"

At Ray's cocked eyebrow, June gave him a crooked grin. "Mr. Osborne's words. From one of his letters."

Like the second floor, the third-floor landing opened onto a large sitting area, complete with a fireplace and a selection of Queen Anne furnishings. A closed door opposite the staircase provided entrance into a hall lined with bedrooms. A narrow window on the far wall allowed in a smattering of light through a lace curtain, and June crossed to a table and snapped on a lamp.

Nothing happened. "Right. No power in the house."

"You did that like it was a habit."

June nodded. "I would come up here to read sometimes, especially if JR was gone or busy with folks downstairs. Sometimes I'd just stare out the windows at the countryside." She let out a long wistful sigh. "I did this, this arrangement. David kept most of the furnishings the way they were."

Ray remembered the controversy that had erupted in the church following JR's death. The house had been renovated and redecorated with church funds, even though JR and June had handled everything, including the purchase of all furnishings. The church board had wanted everything to remain for the next pastor, while a small faction thought June should not be turned out alone and homeless. The decision to allow her to take a few things to put into the small cottage she'd purchased with JR's life insurance had created a lot of dissent, but it had been the main reason June had stayed with the church.

Ray watched as she ran a finger along the back of a love seat, realizing for the first time that June had lost her home and family twice. He felt the stab of an ancient pain as he remembered his wife's death after her long struggle with cancer. He'd barely survived, yet June had gone through it twice. *Too much for one lifetime.*

June suddenly stiffened, as if indulging in memories

disturbed her. She pointed toward the door. "The bathroom is down the hall, third door on the right."

She strode in that direction, a renewed determination in her step. "The servants' rooms were small. Up here, they all shared one bathroom. Apparently they had to schedule time in there to reduce conflicts. Mr. Osborne required them all to bathe at least three times a week. He required a level of cleanliness none of them had ever known before."

"I'm beginning to understand why Rosalie wanted to run away."

June laughed as she reached the hall door and tugged on it. The door's snug fit in the frame kept it secure. "Rosalie was the youngest granddaughter. Siegfried was already gone when she came along. I doubt she knew much about him."

June tugged on the door again, and it popped open. "But she may have known about— Whoa!"

June stared down the hall. The smell of decay, which had permeated the house, suddenly strengthened.

Ray's instincts snapped to attention. He put his hand on her shoulder and held her back. "Stay here."

"But I—"

"Stay here." His firm tone froze her words, and Ray edged down the hall, his hand slowly moving to rest on the grip of his gun. He opened and checked the two small bedrooms that came first, then approached the bathroom warily, his senses still on alert.

He pushed open the door, and the stench flooded around him. The bathroom, almost as large as one of the bedrooms, looked spotlessly clean. With dread in his heart, Ray opened the closet.

He saw her legs first, waxen and gray, then the rest of her form, folded and tucked neatly into the corner of the closet. A leather belt still cut tightly into her throat, and above it, the horror of her last moments remained frozen in Kitty Parker's sightless eyes.

EIGHT

June watched from the hall as the coroner finished her rough exam of Kitty's body, then stood to report her findings to Ray, who lingered in the door frame with a furious expression on his face. Behind them, Jeff Gage dusted every surface in the bathroom for prints, glancing occasionally at Ray, worry clouding his face.

"She's been dead maybe twenty-four to thirty hours." The coroner straightened and rubbed her lower back.

June's stomach tightened at the thought of Kitty's gentle, sweet-spirited husband—they hadn't been married long, and both had waited a long time to find the perfect mate.

She knew how he felt.

"And this isn't your primary crime scene." The coroner glanced at Jeff's work.

"No doubt." His face tensed and his lips thinned to a bare line as he tried to contain his rage. June understood. After all, the house was thoroughly searched after the murder and had been under guard ever since. How had Kitty's body gotten into the house? The tunnel? And her poor husband, not knowing where she was all this time.

"Has anyone told her husband?" June's voice rasped in her throat, like a raw whisper.

Ray nodded. "I contacted the Franklin police chief. Her husband filed a missing persons report this morning, since she never made it home last night."

He looked back at the coroner. "Any defensive wounds?"

She pointed at Kitty's hands. "There's some skin under her nails, some bruising. No signs of a sexual assault."

"Small comfort."

She nodded, and they moved out into the hall as she motioned for her aides to load the body into a bag and onto a gurney. "I'll know more when I can do a thorough exam."

"Thanks. Let me know."

Ray stepped toward June and opened his mouth to speak when Daniel interrupted from down the hall. "Boss?" Ray turned, scowling, as Daniel's eager steps brought him closer. "They found the SUV." He stopped in front of Ray.

"Where?"

"The quarry. Someone drove it off the south end, not realizing the water was low this time of year. Landed nose-first on the edge of the water."

"Did you talk to Fred about searching the property?"

"He called us. Heard the crash about an hour ago, after the attack here."

"Get a warrant for the SUV."

"What about relying on probable cause?"

"With the number of SUVs registered in Bell County? Get the warrant. I don't want a defense attorney questioning the details. Send a team and tell them to find the bullets I put into it. That'll confirm it's the right vehicle and will give validity to the other evidence."

"I'll head over after I get the warrant—"

"Wait. First tell me how this happened."

"What?"

Ray pointed back toward the crime scene. "How did a body get into this house with both doors under guard? Did either of you leave?"

Daniel stiffened. "No, sir. We were here all night." His brow furrowed for a moment. "I mean, Brent was alone for a while before I got here, and he couldn't cover both doors at once, but I got here before dark."

"What about the tunnel? You sealed it. Has it been tampered with?"

"I'll check it now." Daniel did a crisp about-face and left.

June leaned heavily against the wall during the exchange, watching the two men carefully. She'd slept the night before, but the roller coaster of adrenaline, the nonstop ride of events, made even her bones feel achy. The soreness in her right shoulder and hip was the result of Ray slinging her to the ground, and June would have loved to take a couple of aspirin and go to bed. But Ray needed her, and she knew that alone would keep her on her feet.

Ray had been on the same ride but showed little of the strain. His back remained military stiff and his uniform still held its starched and formed creases, despite the tumble they'd taken. The arm he'd wrapped around her in the butler's pantry had been an iron vise like nothing she'd ever felt.

JR had been a big man, almost six foot six and 250 pounds, a thundering, powerful presence in the pulpit and a man no one crossed in the soup kitchens. But JR's biggest strength had been his charisma, his personality. His muscles had never held the might that Ray's lean frame did.

Clearly, when Ray promised to protect her, he'd meant every syllable.

As Daniel turned and left, a resigned expression settled on Ray's face and some of the anger drained away. Ray checked Jeff's progress, then came to June's side, watching as the coroner's team wheeled Kitty Parker's body down the hall.

"You believe him?" June whispered, even though she could see on his face that he trusted his young deputy.

Ray nodded. "He's good. They all are. They wouldn't have missed a body in the search. The only explanation is that it happened during the transition, while Brent was here alone and some of the crowd still mingled out back. Someone came in through the tunnel, maybe the front."

"With a body?"

Ray shrugged one shoulder. "Kitty's petite. I've seen bodies in suitcases, trunks, once even a large duffel bag." He turned to her, keeping his voice low and confidential. "What's supposed to be in Rosalie's diaries?"

June's eyes widened. "You think the diaries have something to do with Kitty's murder?"

"I don't think it's a coincidence that her body was stuffed into the same closet where the diaries were supposedly found. When did David find them?"

June glanced again at the list, now damp from being clutched in her hand for the past few hours, even though she didn't have to look. Standing in the hall, June had memorized every line of the document. "Eight months ago."

"So this discovery of the diaries coincides with when he started letting everything around the house go downhill."

"Yes."

"Tell me everything you know about those diaries, whether it's conjecture, rumor or fact."

June closed her eyes. She and JR had arrived in White Hills long after Rosalie Osborne had vanished, and they'd renovated the house more than twenty years after her disappearance. But June had done her own research into the Osbornes and the house after JR had found Siegfried's letters.

She took a deep breath, trying to organize it in her head, and began slowly.

"Siegfried Osborne joined his father in the banking industry when he was only eighteen years old. When the 1893 panic hit, the family lost everything, and his father committed suicide, which left Siegfried, who was already fearful and eccentric, even more paranoid. He brought the family to Nashville, but even as the economy recovered, Siegfried's mind did not. He moved to White Hills and built this house, becoming almost a recluse."

"What does this have to do—"

June held up a hand. "Bear with me. Siegfried continued to operate an import business out of his home, rebuilding the Osborne wealth. He may have been eccentric, but he also had an incredible head for business. His older son, Eulis, served and died in World War I. The other, Montgomery, wasn't born until much later, but he became an invalid after a hunting accident. Montgomery's first wife left him a few years later. Monty remarried in his late forties, a local girl a lot younger than he was, and she had Rosalie in 1965.

"Beautiful Rosalie enchanted everyone. She inherited her grandfather's intelligence, business sense and, unfortunately, his paranoia. Her solution was to watch everything closely, record everything in her diaries. Apparently, she didn't miss a thing."

"Now, this is all rumor, right?"

June squinted up at him. "The stuff about the financial crisis I found in the state archives in Nashville when I researched the property. Here in the house, we found three different maids' diaries, one from the early part of the twentieth century, just after the house was built, and two from the sixties and seventies. One maid had worked for all three generations.

"They discussed some of 'Miss Rosalie's' observations as well. They were amazed at her evaluations of folks here in Bell County. In fact, she saved one of her servants from marrying a really horrible man, and they listened to her after that, even though she wasn't much more than a kid."

"So we can take that much as fact."

"I think so."

"You think something she observed caused her disappearance?"

June shrugged again. "I just don't know. Without the diaries, I can't do much more than speculate."

"So speculate a bit."

June nodded. "We started renovating the house, and folks who'd known the Osbornes came out of the woodwork. There were times it felt like every female over fifty wanted me to sit down over sweet tea and gingersnaps so we could talk about Rosalie. She graduated early from high school in 1983 and finished a business degree at Yale in only three years. By 1986, at the age of twenty-one, she had taken over the family import business, continuing to run it out of this house. She was beautiful, rich, smart and powerful. The business put her in contact with equally rich and powerful men, and she began a series of affairs best called unfortunate."

"So she was smart and rich but still only twenty-one."

"Exactly. A kid who should have been hanging out

with her friends and having fun instead found herself in the company of Nashville's elite 'old boy network.' Plus she'd just lost her dad, who seemed to have been a good influence on her. Not a good mix."

"And?"

"And…in 1986, she called the sheriff's office, then disappeared."

"You think she named names in the diaries?"

June shrugged one more time. "But here's one for your argument that Rosalie ran away. According to one of my tea-and-snaps ladies, Rosalie dismissed all her live-in help a few months before she vanished. In fact, she dismissed them not long after Monty died. Kept only one girl who came in twice a week."

"That sounds like money problems."

"Could be. Or a desire for more privacy."

Jeff Gage signaled Ray from inside the bathroom, and the sheriff joined his deputy inside the tiled room. They spoke a few moments, then Gage began packing up his kit.

Ray motioned for June to join him, and she pushed away from the wall, nodding at Jeff as he left.

"Ready to check that niche David claims to have found?" Ray stood aside and pushed the closet door open wide. "You're the hidden niche expert."

As June stepped into the closet, she thought back to the day that JR had found that tin box he'd refused to let her examine. When she'd given a playful pout about it, JR had turned sour and critical, cautioning her that the papers concerned current members of the congregation, information that needed to remain confidential. He'd declared his intent to destroy them.

"You have to trust me, June." That's what he said. And I did.

But...do I still?

Unlike modern homes, with rooms made with drywall and metal or wooden studs, the Victorian had been walled with plaster or wood paneling. All the closets were lined with cedar planks inset in beveled frames. Siegfried had put a lot of money into the home, intending it to last for generations.

June felt along the edge of the cedar planks, tapping lightly with her fingernails, then up the edge of the beveled frames.

Almost at eye level, one of the taps turned hollow. June pushed on a cedar plank and felt it give slightly. Taking a deep breath, she slid her thumbnail into the crack between the frame and the edge of the board and pried outward. It resisted at first, but with her second attempt, the board creaked and swung outward on hidden hinges. Ray passed her his flashlight, but the deep pocket revealed only a dark, empty space.

"Nothing." June didn't try to hide her disappointment as she returned the flashlight and started to shut the niche.

"Wait." Ray took the light from her but turned it back toward the plank door. He stepped forward and ran the beam around the edge of the door, pausing it on a small, oval-shaped brown stain on the narrowest side. "I don't think that's a natural part of the wood grain."

An odd lurch of excitement tightened June's stomach as Ray looked down at her. "We need to catch Jeff before he leaves with that kit. I think that's blood."

"Definitely blood." Jeff Gage examined the end of a swab, watching it change colors. "And human. I'll get it to the lab, ask them to rush a comparison with Pastor David."

"Thanks, Jeff." Ray turned to June, who rocked back and forth on her heels, chewing her lower lip.

"This is all about the diaries!" June said suddenly.

"How do you mean?" he asked.

"Well, if that's David's blood, then it got up here after he died. And so did Kitty. Daniel was right. They didn't miss her."

"How so?"

"Kitty must have known that David found the diaries. If she told the wrong person that he'd found them, it may have set this all in motion. They had to make sure David never revealed anything in the diaries. He was killed to keep him silent. She might have been killed either after she told where they were or because she wouldn't tell at all. The killer used Kitty to get to David." June brightened visibly. "Which could mean that David wasn't into anything sordid after all! He could have been trying to sort stuff out and protect the diaries and the information inside! He was just in the way."

Ray crossed his arms. "Or Kitty could have been using the information to blackmail someone, which got her killed."

June's enthusiasm waned a bit. "Or David was black-mailing someone."

"Or maybe this involved no blackmail at all. Kitty and David both tried to keep the information silent, to protect the diaries, and both were killed as a result. The blood is right where the diaries were supposedly hidden. What if David moved them and the killer found the same empty hole that we did?"

June grew still, then pointed at Ray. "I like that idea best."

"Because you don't want to think about Kitty or David involved in blackmail."

"True, but that doesn't mean it's a bad idea, just because I want to believe the best of them."

"Also true."

"So what now?"

Ray reached for her arm and turned her toward the end of the hall. "I need to go over to Fred's quarry and check on the progress with the SUV."

"What about me?"

"You're coming with me."

June stopped. "Isn't that a little open and exposed, given how many times we've been shot at in the last twenty-four hours?"

"Yes, which is why I'm putting you in a vest and not letting you out of my sight."

"I'd be safer here, looking through the hiding places."

"Clearly not, considering we were just shot at. And I can't let you look for evidence alone."

"Why not?"

Ray sighed. "This house is a crime scene, and anything in it is potentially evidence. Anyone not involved in law enforcement can't handle it without supervision."

"Deputize me."

Ray almost laughed. "It doesn't work that way. Besides, you're a witness."

"Which is why you won't let me out of your sight."

"One of the reasons, yes."

June paused, her expression softening. "*One* of the reasons?"

The military-trained, straight-shooting part of Ray's personality flared, and he faced June square, taking her hands in his. "June, you know I'm a no-nonsense man. I care deeply about you. I have for a long time now. I'm going to protect you, and not just because you're a witness. Are we square?"

June's face reddened as she grinned. "Ray Taylor, I've never been romanced more honestly in my life."

He took her elbow and turned her toward the exit again. "Flowers and candy will come later. Just don't expect a new Corvette."

"How about a Jeep instead?"

"That I can swing."

"And it's practical."

"I'm all about the practical."

"I'm not surprised."

After replacing the crime-scene tape over the doors of the house, Ray popped the trunk on his cruiser and pulled out a bulletproof vest, which he helped June into. As he watched her pull the Velcro straps tight, he couldn't help but think that June had changed her mind about a possible relationship with him. Even yesterday, as they'd headed to the hospital, she'd seemed reluctant to be more than friends. But something had clearly shifted. Why?

Was it that he'd proved he could protect and stand by her?

Ray held the door for June as she got in, then he got behind the wheel, pushing the questions to the back of his mind. Whatever it was that had happened, he'd take it. No questions asked.

As he backed out of the driveway, Ray refocused on the case, on finding out who'd killed David Gallagher and Kitty Parker—and protecting the beautiful woman at his side. For now, nothing else mattered.

NINE

An odd warmth settled around June as they headed for the quarry, which she knew came from much more than the weight of the Kevlar vest. She wasn't quite sure why she'd pressed Ray the way she had, but in the past twenty-four hours, she'd felt something deep inside shift. She couldn't quite put her finger on it yet.

She turned to look out the window as Ray drove. *What are You doing with me, Lord? What is this work in my heart?*

June closed her eyes. It was a JR type of prayer, a "tiny cry on the fly," as her husband had called them. When she'd first started hanging out at JR's soup kitchen near downtown Nashville, June had known nothing about God or Christ or faith of any kind. JR had taught her about Jesus and the Bible, but most of all, he'd taught her to turn to God all hours of the day and night, saying quick prayers for help, guidance or thanks. JR had shown her how to praise God in the midst of fear and be in awe of His mighty works.

"No matter how devastating life seems to get," JR

had once told her, "God never fails. When things come together under His reckoning, no power on earth can stand in the face of His works."

June believed it. This lesson had pulled her off the streets and into JR's arms. It had held her up as she remade herself into a pastor's wife and comforted her when she became a pastor's widow.

"You never fail," she whispered.

"What?"

June blinked, then looked at Ray. "God never fails. He won't let us down. He'll show us where to go and what needs to be done."

Ray remained silent, staring at the road, and June returned her gaze to the window, watching the homes of White Hills give way to the fields and wooded acres of rural Bell County. Good county roads narrowed and turned rough, pavement dissolving to gravel, as Ray headed for the privately owned quarry of Fred Whitaker.

Three decades ago, the quarry had produced limestone blocks for local buildings and crushed gravel for roads, but in the early seventies, one end of the quarry abruptly opened up into one of the sinkholes common in northern Middle Tennessee. The underground stream that caused it flooded most of the quarry and made continued excavation expensive and dangerous. The company that owned it sold the property to Fred, who let the water rise.

The quarry filled about halfway up the tall cliffs of its sides, creating a five-acre, 125-foot-deep lake with a narrow gravel shore around the water. One of the remaining truck ramps from the cliffs into the quarry provided access to the water, and Fred charged local scuba divers twenty dollars a day to explore. Local dive shops had started doing their open-water certifications at the quarry, and Fred, now close to eighty years old, suddenly found himself with a money-making enterprise. He called it Serendipity Lake. Everyone else just called it "Fred's quarry."

Ray waved at Fred, who sat under an umbrella near the ramp's entrance, then eased the cruiser down the long ramp and parked on the shore. The shoreline along the western and northern edges of the quarry remained visible year-round, but the southern and eastern shores could only be seen in the height of summer or, like this year, during a dry spring. The rest of the year, they remained submerged, with the clear spring waters against the high cliffs of the quarry.

"There it is." June pointed to the south, where a cluster of officers stood around a black SUV, which had plowed through the bushes at the top of the cliff and plummeted nearly seventy feet to land, grille down, on the gravel shore. The impact had shattered the grille and popped the hood, which now formed an accordioned A shape over the motor. Gravity and the slight slope of the shore had caused it to rock backward on its wheels, causing the back tires to blow. The side panels had been thrust backward, causing them to crumple and dent.

"It looks sad."

Ray glanced at June. "It's a truck."

June sniffed at him. "You know what I mean."

As they got out and headed toward the crash, June spotted Daniel scooting from under the SUV, flashlight in hand.

Daniel snapped around, looking pleased with himself. "It's definitely the SUV you took a shot at." He headed for Ray and June, his shoes crunching loudly on the gravel. "There's a bullet hole in the seat but no round. He must have dug it out. But there's one in the firewall. He also tried to remove all the VINs, but he forgot the one on the radiator bracket."

"Did you find anything else?"

"Yeah, I think the attack on the house may have been a last-minute deal when the bomb didn't achieve its... objective." He glanced at June quickly, then continued. "He got sloppy, maybe improvising. There are tread marks near the church that look like a match to these tires, and two shell casings. He also backed into a post at the church while speeding out, and the paint will probably be from this vehicle."

"No doubt. Could be why he decided to dump it. Anything in the glove box?"

"Nada. He even removed the owner's manual."

"So I'm guessing no fingerprints?"

Daniel shook his head. "Maybe we can get something off the VIN, provided it's not stolen. I'm sure he didn't bother too much under the hood since he thought it was going under the water and wouldn't be found for a while."

Ray looked up, studying the overgrown brush that ringed the edges of the quarry cliffs.

Daniel studied his boss a moment. "You think he's watching us?"

Ray focused on where the bushes were crushed, where the SUV had gone over. "No. The bedrock here pushes through the dirt, makes it very hard going on foot, and an ATV or off-road truck would create an echo. We have the only access road covered. He'd be too exposed, too easy to find. He wouldn't take the chance."

"Then what?"

Ray's thoughtful gaze turned on June, which made a slight shiver eke up her spine.

"What?" she whispered.

"He took out the computer. His only remaining target seems to be June, and with us all around her, a blitz isn't going to work."

"So he's going to ground."

Ray nodded at Daniel's words, but his eyes remained on June. "His next attack will be stealthier."

Ray watched June as his words sank in. At first, fear clouded her eyes, then she looked straight up and mumbled something under her breath. When she looked down again, she began peeling back the Velcro on her vest.

"What are you doing?" He reached to stop her, but she moved away.

"I won't live in fear, Ray." June pulled the vest away from her body. "This guy is a marksman. He hit a moving car from up on that ridge and a computer through a window, probably from more than two hundred yards away. The vest will just make him aim for my head."

"Which is easier to miss. That's the point!" Ray fought the urge to tackle June and force her back into the vest.

"Easier, but not impossible. He's not going to come at me hand-to-hand with a knife or a pistol."

"June, we don't *know* what he'll do next."

She held the vest out to Ray. "Take it. It doesn't matter what he does. It matters what I choose to do, and I choose to trust God and you. Do you have much left to do here?"

"I've already called for a tow to get it out of here and to a garage," Daniel said.

Ray nodded. "Fine. Then you get some rest. That's an order." He turned back to June. "Why did you ask?"

June rolled her shoulders back, as if relieved to have the vest off them. "One, I'm hungry. It's been a long time since that skimpy hospital breakfast. Two, I want to stop by my house and grab my laptop. That bullet shattered the screen of the parsonage computer and part of the case, but there's a chance the hard drive is still intact. Even if it isn't, David kept a lot of stuff on backup disks. It's already getting dark. I want to get back to the parsonage before it's too late."

She glanced quickly at Daniel, then back to Ray as she gestured at the car. "This guy may be the shooter, but you don't really think he's the one after the information—or me—do you?"

Ray cleared his throat and his voice dropped. "As we discussed, there were two people in the house when you got there."

She took a deep breath. "I saw the second set of footprints again when I was in the house this morning. This time I looked closer. Narrow heels that barely left a dot of blood. Pointed toes."

Ray and Daniel looked at each other and then back at June. Ray shook his head in disbelief, trying not to smile at June's newfound detective skills.

"High heels," June finished. "But judging by the amused looks on your faces, I'm guessing you already knew that the other killer in the house was a woman."

The scent of the crispy grilled steak wafted up to June, almost as savory as the taste of the juicy ribeye. She dug into her meal with gusto, watching Ray from under half-lidded eyes.

Ray had disappeared into his head, silent on the drive back into White Hills. He'd taken her to purchase a new cell phone, then to the City Diner, one of the cultural hearts of the small town, but now he scowled at his pork chops and pushed the plate away. He sipped his coffee idly, his gaze focused out the window on some far place.

June watched him a few moments, then paused to drink a bit of her sweet tea. "I thought you'd be famished."

He remained silent a moment, then answered slowly, still looking out the window. "I never ate much on patrol. Or during the initial heat of a case."

"What did Anne fix for you?"

"Soup. Light. Something nourishing I could drink on the run." June waited silently, watching to see how long it would take for what she'd said to sink in.

Not as long as she'd expected. Only seconds passed until he blinked twice, assessed the exchange, then refocused his eyes on her. "Why did you ask about Anne?"

June swallowed another sip of tea. "I know we moved here after she'd passed, but you can't think I haven't heard about her." She paused, then shrugged one shoulder. "Especially after you started sitting with me at church. You can't imagine how many times I've been compared to her."

Ray's mouth twitched in amusement. "Actually, I can. What do they say most often?"

"That she was perfect. And I'm not."

Ray reached for his coffee. "Yet neither is true. What else?"

June took another bite of steak, glad that he was talking to her again. "They honestly don't understand how you could be interested in me after having Anne as a wife. 'Like serving mud pie after caviar,' one of the ladies said."

A laugh burst from Ray. June sat straighter and put down her fork. "I didn't find it that funny."

Ray wiped his mouth with a napkin, his eyes gleaming. "But it is. If you only knew."

"So tell me."

He twisted in the chair to face her directly. "All right. Anne was gentle but tough and no-nonsense. She spoke softly because she grew up with a dad who worked nights and slept days. She inherited doilies from her grandmother and her backbone from her grandfather, who was a long-haul trucker before the interstates existed. When I was elected sheriff, a lot of the society ladies around here wanted to pull her into their midst, but she preferred teaching kindergarten, which took up most of her time."

"So she kept them at arm's length."

"They think she was 'perfect' because she refused to engage in any of their gossip and games, yet she never criticized them. She avoided them, which they interpreted as being the good wife who stayed at home with her husband."

"But she was no milquetoast."

He grinned. "Anne had strength no one outside got to see. Don't let anyone tell you Anne had a sweet, patient temperament." Ray paused. "The two of you have more in common than people realize. You're just—"

"Louder?"

"Oh, yeah. And more determined. Anne would step around trouble and ignore it, if she could. You plant your feet, stand your ground and get in its face. Especially if it's a threat to your…" His voice trailed off.

"My what?"

Ray hesitated, watching her closely, and June felt a twinge of anxiety. *Oh, this must be bad.* June took a deep breath to brace herself. "Just say it, Ray."

He looked up, his face darker, and June got the feeling he wished he hadn't started down this path. "You have this thing about being JR's wife."

She blinked, not sure she'd heard correctly. "And?" she prompted.

His eyes narrowed. "You never introduce yourself without adding, 'I'm JR Eaton's wife.'"

June put down her fork. "What's wrong with that?"

Ray's brow furrowed. "To start with, you're June. You're not just JR's wife. You're independent, strong, caring. Smarter than most people I know. In a few years, June, most people around here aren't going to remember who JR was. That's the way life is."

A fearful sense of desperation gripped June's stomach, and she leaned forward. "That's not true. He transformed this town. He made that church. He made me!" She pointed at her own chest, emphasizing her point with a sharp poke. "You can't tell me people will forget him, forget what he's done, forget what he did for me. I was nothing without him!"

"Didn't you once tell me that we are all known to God for who we are in our hearts? In our souls? We aren't what someone else made us. We're what God makes us."

June pushed her chair back from the table, fury heating her face as she stood up. "Don't you *dare* use my own words against me."

The waitress approached them, her hands gesturing for June to lower her voice. "Please. Mrs. Eaton. Can I get you anything?"

June pointed at the waitress, still glaring at Ray. "See? 'Mrs. Eaton.' Some people remember!" June shook her head angrily. "But I guess not for long, if I listen to you. If I still had a purse, I'd ask for separate checks, but even *that's* gone. It's *all* gone!"

June pivoted on one foot and stormed out, not caring who saw the rage on her face or the first tears in her eyes. Leaving the diner, she marched toward the small cottage she now called home, which sat only a few blocks from White Hills' picturesque downtown.

How dare he? Her wrath at Ray put a lock on her chest so tight she could barely breathe. *How dare he tell me how I should see myself? How to behave?*

And what a joke to think I could ever be with him!

June's steps slowed at the thought. No matter what interest he had in her or she in him—how different they were. "What a laugh." June's words, low and dark, released more sadness than she'd felt in a long time. She was a fool for even thinking that his overtures could lead anywhere, that she could open up her heart to another man.

She was JR's wife. She'd been nothing before that. She'd never be anything after that.

Her wrath dissolved into overwhelming sadness, an escalating grief arising that felt like an abyss of darkness. Tears flooded her cheeks, blinding her until she could barely see where to put one foot in front of the other.

"Didn't you once tell me that we are all known to God for who we are in our hearts? In our souls? We aren't what someone else made us. We're what God makes us."

June sniffed. *My own words. How could he!*

So do you believe them or not?

June wiped her eyes and looked around to get her bearings. She stood on the corner of her own street, realizing she'd almost missed it. She headed west, spotting the pale yellow house with the blue shutters a block away. Only four houses and an alley lay between her and home.

Home. She'd not been home since early yesterday, and the unceasing events of today had carried them almost until dark. Seeing her house made her crave its welcome refuge. June suddenly longed to curl up on her sofa with a soft quilt and a cup of hot tea. Lock out the world, everything. Lock *him* out. Hibernate in her refuge forever.

So do you believe them or not?

June picked up her pace again. Of course, she did. Those words were from one of the first lessons JR had taught her, just before he told her she had great potential.

If God loves us as we are, why would He want us to change? Of course, He wants the best for us, to use our gifts from Him to the best of our ability, to live up to the potential He gives us. But does that mean living only as someone else's image of who you should be? If it's a good image, a beneficial image, does it matter if it's not God's image of you, His chosen path?

"Know this," JR had once preached to his entire congregation. "Know that God has said to you, 'You are *my* child.'"

June crossed the alley and then leaned heavily against a signpost. She closed her eyes and turned her face upward. "Please tell me," she whispered. "Show me what to do."

Suddenly she heard the low growl of an engine dropping into gear. June spun around, eyes flying open as headlights snapped on, blinding her from down the street. A car plunged forward, bounced up on the sidewalk and headed straight for her.

TEN

June couldn't even scream as the small red sports car raced toward her like a malicious wildcat on the chase. She turned and fled for the closest house, hoping the front porch would offer some protection. *Any* kind of protection.

She glanced back to see the car closing fast, nearing the alley that ran between the houses of the normally sedate neighborhood. That was when she felt, as well as heard, the thunderous growl of the Bell County sheriff's cruiser that flared from the alley like an avenging warrior.

The black-steel push frame on the front of the cruiser impacted the sports car in a direct T-bone hit, crushing the passenger door. The heavy cruiser jammed the smaller vehicle sideways, tires screeching, until the driver's side collided with a telephone pole on the opposite side of the street. The sound of twisting metal and shattering glass stopped just as abruptly as it began, and Ray leaped from the cruiser, gun drawn.

June's knees gave way and she dropped to the ground,

heart pounding, as she watched Ray crouch behind his door, calling out for the driver to make himself known. At first, the only thing she heard was the harsh rasping of her own frantic breaths, the drumming of her pulse in her ears. Then she heard a faint call from within the sports car. Ray remained on guard, gun aimed, as sirens blared in the distance and the first responders arrived in droves.

The next two hours passed in a blur. At some point, an EMT wrapped her in a warm blanket as she sat in the back of an ambulance, watching the scene, shock keeping her numb and silent. Bright halogen lights on tall poles were erected as the night set in, adding to the unreal nature of the event.

The driver of the sports car surrendered up two guns, including a rifle, before being extracted from the crushed vehicle. As the firefighters lifted him out, June felt a strange disappointment. She'd assumed the sniper would be a man whose build was as menacing as his actions, but her attacker's short, wiry, muscular frame seemed distinctly unimposing. Then he turned and looked at her.

Bright gray eyes glared from beneath a thick, heavily shadowed brow. A beard hid his mouth, but his expression, frozen into a hard mask, held true malevolence. The chill that ran through her made her pull the blanket tighter around her shoulders.

Yet she could not look away, anger and fear blending inside her chest with a deep sorrow. This man had killed David. He'd choked the life from Kitty.

And he wants to kill me. Why? What makes someone do that?

EMTs hefted the man, both legs broken, into an ambulance. The last bits of fear slipped away from her as an officer closed the door and thumped on it, signaling to the driver that he could leave.

No fear. He may have been wicked, even evil, but he was just a man. No match for God. Or even the sheriff of Bell County.

June searched for Ray in the crowd, spotting him giving orders, and watching as a tow truck approached for the sports car. Small and made mostly from fiberglass, the red car would have been deadly to June, but Ray's cruiser had almost demolished it, receiving only minimal damage in return. June could see a few scratches from flying metal and glass, a cracked panel near the motor and a smashed headlight.

Ray turned and saw June watching him. He walked slowly toward her, almost as if he were expecting her to turn away. She didn't, waiting until he stood close before speaking. "This is becoming a habit of yours, isn't it? This saving-my-life thing."

"Just glad I was here," he said, watching her closely.

"Why *were* you here?"

He hesitated, then went on. "I knew you didn't want me to follow you. But I wasn't about to leave you unprotected…" His words faded.

June nearly laughed. "You were trying to sneak down the alley to my house."

"Be glad I was," Ray replied, a hint of a smile in his eyes.

June let out a deep sigh. "You have no idea." She pushed back the blanket, stepped out of the ambulance and put her arms around him. Her move startled Ray and he stiffened at first, then relaxed, folding her into a deep hug. June pressed her cheek against his shirt, relishing the warmth of his chest, the secure strength of his embrace.

After a moment, June leaned back to look into his face. "You've also given me some things to think about. And believe me, I'm going to think about them."

Ray stroked her face with one finger. "So you're not mad anymore?"

"You're joking, right? After this, you think I'd still be mad at you?"

"June, lovely lady, I never second-guess what a woman thinks. I do not, and never will, understand how women think."

In spite of it all, June laughed. An officer interrupted from behind Ray with a crisp, "Sheriff?"

They turned, and June stepped away from Ray, crossing her arms over her stomach.

"Yes?"

The officer handed Ray a paper as he spoke. "The driver refused to talk and he didn't have ID on him. But the car was reported stolen early yesterday morning from a downtown Nashville garage. It's registered to Virginia Bridges."

June felt the hair on her neck prickle. "Virginia Bridges. You mean Hunter's mother?"

Ray nodded, the car's registration clutched in his left hand. "It's the right address."

"Curiouser and curiouser." June paused, then put her hand on Ray's arm. "You know, Virginia Bridges has a preference for stiletto heels."

Ray held up a finger to stop her. "Don't go there. At least not yet."

June smiled. "And you claim not to know how women think."

Ray sat in the dark, watching June's house. The street behind him had been cleared of all vehicles, the glass swept away, sand put over the oil that had drained from the red sports car. Once again, it was a sedate neighborhood street, with its residents going through their nightly routines undisturbed by smashing cars and blaring sirens.

Including June. Two yellow lights glowed from within, casting long shadows on the small, neatly landscaped yard. Early spring flowers lined the sidewalk and flowering shrubs stood guard under the living room and bedroom windows. Floodlights under the eaves illuminated the sides of the house, and Ray had given June strict instructions to leave them on all night.

He could see her shadow moving against the closed blinds, and he imagined her maybe having a last cup of tea before bed, then plucking a favorite book to read.

Ray liked this little cottage, and he was glad she'd

asked him to help her maintain it. It had been in perfect shape when she'd bought it three years ago, but Tennessee's odd weather never was kind to a home, and he'd repaired gutters, replaced shingles, fixed the dryer— whatever she needed.

He'd always admired June for her spirit and dignity but had never thought about her in a romantic way until long after JR's death. Then one day, she'd asked him to change out a light fixture and he'd stayed for coffee afterward. As she'd bustled about the kitchen, Ray had been struck by the soft flow of her hair, the blue eyes that sparkled with intelligence and wit.

Unlike some men, Ray had always been drawn to strong women, the kind who make you think they'd go into battle at your side. June certainly fit that bill. Ray had seen her stand down gossipy committees and annoyed board members. Her reason for being at the parsonage yesterday morning had been believable to him because it was typical of June.

Was it only yesterday?

Ray released a long, exhausted sigh. The weariness in his very bones told him how long the past two days had been. Still, he would not leave June. Daniel would relieve him at midnight, but only as the alert guard. Ray might rest, might even sleep, but he would do it right here, in his car.

He would not leave her.

A chime at his side alerted him to an incoming message on his cell phone, and he checked the brightly lit screen. It was from June.

500 yrs ago, you would have been a knight on a white horse. Thank you. Get some rest. J.

Ray grinned. Well, their courtship had been unusual even before the shooting started.

Courtship. If that was what you could really call it. Part of Ray didn't want to admit exactly how much this woman meant to him. The other part wanted to wrap her in his arms and never let go. Either way, they had to get through this first.

Lord, help us get through this, safe and sound. And preferably soon.

Ray shifted in his seat, pressing down with one foot to release a cramped calf. He hoped that with the capture of the sharp-shooting assailant, June was most likely safe for a while. But if he was just a hired gun, whoever orchestrated this could just hire someone else. Regardless, Ray would not—could not—lower his guard.

Instead, he watched as the last two lights downstairs in the cottage winked out, leaving just the bedroom light on. He then reached for a thermos of coffee and settled in for a long night.

June stared upward, watching the ceiling fan circle slowly and tapping her fingers on her stomach. Her bedtime book, a new mystery by one of her favorite writers, lay abandoned on the bedside table next to her new cell phone, her portable house phone and a can of pepper spray—the last pressed into her hand by the man sitting in the car outside her home.

June had thought sleep would come easily tonight.

Instead, tension overrode exhaustion, and her mind wouldn't stop going over possible reasons behind these attacks. It circled and spun, and the reasons ranged from the simple to the ridiculous. June wondered if it were all making her just a bit paranoid.

When her cell phone chirped, she jumped, then snatched it from the table. She grinned and thumbed her phone open.

Rivers on at 12. Will rest then. What book?

Her smile broadened at his accurate guess, and she tapped in the answer:

Maron's latest. Want a review? Would tell you to give Daniel a hug, but the neighbors might get the wrong idea.

She sent it, imagining his laugh. She liked his laugh, the way it came deep from within his chest and added a sparkle of light to his brown eyes.

Her phone chirped.

Ha! Would be a surprise to April. Maron's good, review later. You are safe. We will unravel more tomorrow. Dream well.

June's grin eased into a gentle smile as she hesitated in responding. Her initial thought came from a rush of emotion unlike any she'd ever known. But she held it in check—it was too soon. Too much chaos enveloped them both.

Guard well, my sweet knight.

With that simple text, June closed her phone and snuggled into the pillows, discovering that she was, in fact, truly exhausted.

ELEVEN

The first light of dawn woke Ray. He opened the door of the cruiser and forced himself to emerge, stiff and sore. He'd slept hard, which he knew would serve him well later, but for now, he felt old and stiff. He stretched, adjusted his clothes, then checked in with Daniel, whose patrol car sat only a few yards away.

The night had been a quiet one, and Ray sent Daniel home to sleep. When Ray called into the station, however, a surprise awaited him. Jeff Gage, who'd slept through last night's events, had already arrived at the office and had been making calls and following up on reports, including one on the fingerprints taken from June's attacker.

"His name is Stephen Webster. Miami PD has a running file on him. Served in Iraq, first in the army then as a civilian security contractor. Now he apparently takes on contracts of an entirely different nature."

"A professional."

"Yep, and not your run-of-the-mill gang hitter, either.

Seems he's known in Florida for leaving some prominent citizens in the Everglades for the gators."

Ray braced himself against his car's trunk, forcing his leg muscles to stretch. His left calf tried to cramp again, and Ray pressed down hard with his toe. "Sounds like a lovely guy."

"They sounded glad to have him out of Florida. They haven't been able to gather enough evidence for a conviction, so they'll be thrilled if we can pin this on him."

"Did you tell them we'd do our best?"

Jeff chuckled. "When I told them Webster spent most of last night in surgery for two broken legs, they suggested we put guards on the surgeons as well as the nurses. They're also sending me what they have so far on his financials. Maybe we can track the money, see who hired him for this."

"If he's a pro, I wouldn't count on it. My guess is it's either cash or through an offshore account. Is he awake yet?"

"Not sure. I talked to the charge nurse on his floor, and she said surgery lasted several hours. You did quite a number on him. They had to put six pins in one of his femurs. He's cuffed to the bed, but he's not going anywhere for a while anyway. How hard did you hit him?"

"I wasn't exactly watching the speedometer."

"I'll go over the car this morning, but my guess is that it'll be as clean as the SUV. Interesting that it's registered to Virginia Bridges."

"More interesting is that she reported it stolen from a Nashville garage before David Gallagher was killed and while Webster was still traipsing around Bell County in a black SUV. Why don't you check with that garage and see if they have security cameras. Find out why the attendants who see Mrs. Bridges drive in and out every day didn't notice when a mean-looking guy with a beard decided to leave with the fancy red car."

"You got it, boss. Anything else?"

Ray hesitated, something tickling the back of his brain. "Jeff, is there anyone around you?"

Gage hesitated, obviously hearing the suspicion in Ray's voice. "Two."

"Were you surprised to see either of them there so early?"

Another hesitation. "Yes."

Ray cleared his throat and stood a bit straighter. "Webster didn't wind up on that ridge over the Springfield highway by coincidence. If anyone asks you, I'm taking June to Nashville to talk to Virginia Bridges. Got it?"

"Yes, sir."

"Text me those two names. And call the phone company. I want the usage details on every line out of the station and everyone's cell phone. Even yours. Understood?"

"Yes, sir."

"Call Judge Hines. You'll have warrants by noon. I'll fill you and Rivers in later. I want to see both of you in my office around four this afternoon."

"We'll be there."

"Thanks. And be careful."

"Yes, sir."

Ray hung up and instantly received Gage's text. When he saw the two names—Carter and Parkinson—his chest tightened. Both had been at the scene last night and should not have been on duty so soon this morning. Their regular shifts didn't start for another hour.

He snapped the phone shut and looked at June's cottage, where the kitchen light glowed through the drawn blinds. The sun had cleared the horizon, but long, deep shadows still mixed deep purples and blues into the rising golds. The air smelled damp and fresh, and a heavy dew coated his shoes as Ray headed for the backyard, which was enclosed by a high privacy fence. Although Webster lay cuffed to a bed, not all the parties in this were under lock and key. Ray wasn't about to take chances with June's life.

He circled the perimeter of the backyard, checking the outside of the fence for tampering and the ground around it for footprints and disturbances. Other than a badly buried hambone, he found nothing. He slowly returned to the front, where he found June sitting on the front porch with two mugs of coffee.

June ran a hand through her hair, still tousled from her night's sleep. "Good morning."

Ray paused at the foot of the front steps. June's cottage, built in the 1940s, had a broad plank porch complete with a swing hanging from the rafters and two cane-bottom rockers. Pots of Boston ferns and petunias hung from the eaves, and window boxes of impatiens stood guard on the rails. June, dressed in a sweat suit and socks, sat in the swing, one foot pushing it slowly back and forth. The mugs sat on a low table between the rockers.

"Want some coffee before you mount your charger for the day?"

"I would love some."

She scooted to her left in the swing. "Bring them. Sit next to me."

Ray picked up the mugs and handed one to her. She stilled the swing while he sat, then resumed the slow push, letting the swing arc slowly under their weight.

"You're up early."

She drank deeply from the mug. "Mrs. Digsby, my neighbor out back, called to tell me some man was prowling around outside my fence."

Ray's face grew warm. "Sorry."

June laughed, a low, soft sound. "Never apologize for taking care of me, Sir Knight." She paused. "I like it."

They sat in silence for a few moments, then Ray took a deep breath. "Gage is going to check on the stolen car report this morning, and I'd like for us—"

"Y'know, I come out here early and just sit, listening to the birds and watching the sun get brighter and brighter. The bluebirds are amazing this time of year, although sometimes I think the mockingbirds are on a campaign to deafen me." She sipped the coffee. "Something about spring mornings reminds me that the world is bigger than my problems and that God takes care of everything."

"June—"

"Do you have a change of uniform in the car?"

Ray hesitated, then nodded. "I keep one in the trunk."

June put a gentle hand on his arm and peered up at him with soft affection in her eyes. "Then before we dive back into the world where people shoot at us and try to run us down with cars, can we sit down to some yummy food and thank God for the good things in our lives?"

Ray hesitated, then nodded. "We do have to eat."

She grinned. "Exactly. Grab the clean uniform, then you can take a shower while I start breakfast."

When Ray returned to the house, he discovered she already had biscuits in the oven and was carefully separating the eggs for an omelet. His eyebrows arched. "Exactly how early *did* you get up?"

She shrugged one shoulder, then tossed another eggshell into a small bucket on the counter. "Long before Mrs. Digsby called. I wasn't joking about the mockingbirds. There's one in residence in a bush outside my window who's more annoying than a rooster. I've already had my shower. Just still need to do the hair-and-makeup thing."

"How about if, after we eat, I clean the kitchen while you do that?"

June grinned. "Deal." She leaned over to check the oven timer. "You've got about ten minutes before the biscuits come out. There's a new razor in the medicine cabinet you can use."

"I'm on it." Ray headed down the hall to June's bathroom. Even though he'd been in this house a number of times, Ray never failed to be impressed with how carefully every item had been positioned. Even pictures, some of which he'd helped her hang, were in a precisely measured spot on the chosen wall. He never spotted a speck of dust or a cobweb anywhere in the house.

Ray wondered if such cleanliness was a reaction to the squalor of her youth, her dependence on the image of the perfect pastor's wife...or just because she tended to be a bit of a neat freak. It had almost become a challenge to him, to find something out of place, maybe a dust bunny under a chair.

Why do you keep looking for flaws in her?

Interesting question, and one he'd asked himself before. Maybe because it was the flaws, the "little imperfections," that Ray found most interesting in people. His was a job that dwelled on human frailties, and he'd come to expect that everyone had them. Even more, he'd come to distrust people who tried to hide them.

It was one of the reasons that the "perfect" label that some people in the community had placed on his wife amused him deeply. Obviously, their memories of her were faulty if they couldn't remember the temper that she controlled only in the classroom. Or the frequent fender benders that kept their insurance rate through the roof.

Nor was Anne physically perfect. They'd forgotten

that a childhood injury to her hips had left her with a constant limp. And they'd used that injury to explain why they were childless to hide the real reason for their choice, a secret that Ray kept even all these years after her death.

Children.

Ray turned on the hot water, trying to push away thoughts of the past. Past events. Past regrets. Dwelling on such tended to be a waste of time. Focus on the right now…the future. The past was set in stone, whereas the present grew beneath your feet. And the future consisted of dreams to pursue.

Ray paused, realizing in that moment that the idea of having children with June made up one of the most pleasant and satisfying dreams of the future he'd had in a long time.

He broke free of the fantasy with a sharply inhaled breath. *Better focus on the present, Ray, old boy. Thoughts of the future are the last thing you need right now.*

June hummed a lullaby as she pulled the pan of biscuits from the oven, a comforting melody that reminded her of the nursery in JR's downtown ministry. So many homeless families had small children or infants that made it hard for the parents to search for jobs. JR had set up a day care and June had helped out, learning for the first time how much she enjoyed taking care of babies.

Those were good days. Before we married. Before White Hills. When we just focused on helping others.

June lifted the lid on her skillet, checking on the omelets, which were browning slowly but steadily. Small morsels of cheese had slipped out around the edges and toasted nicely in the oil, blending sweetly with the other scents of breakfast—biscuits, gravy, fresh fruit, bacon.

June set a bowl of fruit on the table next to the plate of biscuits, then expertly served up the fluffy omelets and bacon. Ray emerged just as she put the plates on the placemats, looking infinitely more refreshed.

"Wow, you look better."

Ray's eyes widened in mock surprise, and he placed his palm over his heart. "Well, thank you. I think."

June smiled. "You slept in your car, and trust me—you looked and smelled like you'd slept in your car."

"Job hazard. This, on the other hand, smells awesome."

"Thank April. She lived with JR and me for a while after her divorce. Taught me how to make an omelet that will melt in your mouth. Sit. Will you say grace?"

"I'd be honored."

They sat, clasped hands and Ray spoke a clear prayer to God that reached right into June's heart.

"Lord, we give You thanks today that we are here to serve You. We praise Your gifts to us and ask for Your guidance as we deal with what lies in front of us. Thank You for bringing this lady into my life, and thank You for our friendship. Please watch over and care for us this day and in the future, and bless this food to the nourishment of our bodies. All this we ask in Your name. Amen."

June squeezed Ray's hands before releasing them. "That was a great prayer."

"Thanks." He smiled almost shyly, then dug eagerly into his omelet.

"So what are the plans for today?"

He looked up, swallowed and his eyes brightened. "Today," he announced, "we discover how Rosalie Osborne's diaries caused David Gallagher's death."

TWELVE

June stared at the grand old Victorian, which no longer bore any resemblance to the welcoming, charming home she and JR had created. The bomb and the bullets had scarred and ripped the eastern side of the house. The darkened paint, shattered electric meter and torn boards made the entire house appear to list to the right, like a tall ship wounded near the port keel.

"It's okay," June whispered. "We can make you whole again."

Ray cut his eyes toward her but remained silent, a smile teasing the corners of his mouth. He opened the cruiser door and got out, heading for the back door.

June grabbed the backpack holding her laptop and followed him. She stepped around the reddish-brown footprints on the porch, scowling. "Are we going to talk to Virginia Bridges?"

"One thing at a time."

"She's rich. She could run off to St. Kitt's or something."

"A. She's just a victim of car theft. She's not officially a suspect."

"Yet."

"B. Her son is in the middle of a major campaign. No way she'd bolt from that without good reason."

June sniffed at the lingering scent of decay in the house. "In other words, you're going to get to her last."

"Unless we turn up direct evidence about her, yes."

"If we find them, can you fingerprint Rosalie's diaries?"

Turning to look at her, Ray stopped so suddenly June almost plowed into him. June stepped backward, regaining her balance. Ray's eyes were intense. "Why did you ask that? What do you have in mind?"

June stared back at him. "Promise you won't laugh."

"No promise. Just tell me."

June straightened her shoulders. "Okay. Going on the premise that David found the diaries…"

"Yes."

"Look, if I recorded that much of my life, then there's no way I'd run away from home and leave my diaries behind. They'd be in my suitcase along with my passport and a lot of cash."

Ray grew more intrigued. "So?"

"So if she didn't take them, then she most likely didn't leave voluntarily. What if whoever took her did so because he knew about the diaries? Maybe even touched them at some point before she hid them? Can fingerprints last twenty-five years?"

Ray's brow furrowed. "Depends."

"Where do you want to start?"

"You start with the laptop. I'll start with the niches on this floor." Ray pulled the list from his pocket.

June turned toward the butler's pantry. "Let me know if you find the Holy Grail."

Ray chuckled, and June turned her attention to the wrecked computer. "Like old-home week," she murmured, her hands gently pulling apart the splintered remains of the case. Odd, distant memories flashed through her mind as she pulled a set of small tools from her backpack to help her dismantle what was left of the computer's case.

Back in her hacker days, she'd rescued the hard drive from many a damaged computer. Like most people who take out their frustration on a computer, the sniper had aimed for the screen, one of the least essential parts. Now, peeling away the disjointed case, June extracted the hard drive, which appeared intact. Having left her own hard drive at home, June opened her laptop and installed the drive from the parsonage computer.

The parsonage computer was an older model, but the same brand as hers. Holding her breath, June powered up her laptop. The drive purred like a stroked kitten, and start-up images popped up on the screen. "Yes!"

Ray poked his head into the pantry. "It works?"

"Just like it's supposed to. You find anything yet?"

"Lots of empty spaces, but according to the list, they were empty when discovered."

June nodded, still watching the computer. "Most were, like I mentioned yesterday. What I didn't get a chance to tell you was that one of the maids mentioned in her diary that Rosalie's father, Monty, had sold a lot of Siegfried's prized possessions. The maid had been really loyal to Siegfried, and she complained about Monty's lack of respect for all his father had achieved. She mentioned a set of silver coins, some jewelry. My guess is that Monty emptied a lot of the niches himself."

Ray's eyes narrowed. "Combined with Rosalie's firing of the help, it sounds as if the Osbornes had financial problems again."

June nodded, clicking open several of the numbered files. "Rosalie took over the family business before Monty died. Maybe his mind had led him to making some foolish decisions."

"And schizophrenia can be inherited."

June turned to look at Ray, whose gaze had grown distant as he stared out the broken window. "What do you mean?"

Ray focused on her again. "You said Siegfried suffered from extreme paranoia. Heard voices in the walls and had obsessive tendencies. He sounds like a paranoid schizophrenic to me."

June realized where Ray was headed with this. "If he did, then Monty might have had the same illness."

"And he'd seen his father lose everything before."

"So if Rosalie had returned from college to find her father selling off the family heirlooms…"

"It might have driven her to take over the business and push to make it successful."

"Or to marry into money."

Ray's eyes narrowed. "All those 'unfortunate' affairs."

June nodded, then gestured toward the list in his hand. "Read me the contents summary for each niche. Let's see if the computer files still match."

Ray smoothed the wrinkled sheet out against the wall. "The ones on this floor are numbered seven through fifteen. All empty on the list and in reality."

"Right. No files for those."

"One through six, in the basement. Only one with contents, number five. A set of silver candlesticks."

June checked the corresponding computer document. "Right. They were there when we opened that one. We donated them to the Bell County museum, so it should be empty now."

Ray continued to read the contents from the list. All matched the files on the computer, until he came to a niche located in the family nursery. "Date book."

June opened the corresponding file and froze. "Oh, no."

Ray peered over her shoulder. "What?"

Silently, she pointed to the screen. The entry read simply, "JR's date book, tin box."

"Why would JR hide a date book?"

June shook her head, feeling suddenly chilled. "He

didn't. He wouldn't—" Her voice cracked. She shook her head and cleared her throat. "Look at when this file was modified. This has to be David's entry."

"Let's go."

They headed up the stairs, almost breaking into a run as they moved down the hall to the room that had once been the Osborne family nursery. Ray closed the door and June dropped to her knees behind it, using her fingernails to pry a section of baseboard away from the wall. It resisted at first, then gave way with a sharp creak, and June pulled it from the dovetailed groves it rested in.

"Hand me your flashlight."

Ray pulled his light from his belt and June snapped on the light. As she peered deep into the crevice, her heart sank as she saw what lay within. She pressed her cheek against the floor, feeling the first tears welling up in her eyes. "How could you?" she whispered.

"June?" Ray's deep voice was full of concern.

Her fingers shaking, June reached into the dark niche, pulling out a leather-covered date book, a small shoe box…and a dusty black tin box with a faded red rose on the cover. She passed everything to Ray, straightened and leaned back on her heels, her chest tight as the tears leaked down her cheeks.

"He'd promised to get rid of it." She reached out toward the box, but Ray's hand closed around her wrist.

"I want Jeff to fingerprint everything inside before we examine them."

June pulled from his grasp, staring at the box. "He asked me to trust him. Why would he keep it? Why did he lie?" The very air in the room suddenly felt heavy, crushing in on her, and she pushed to her feet. "I have to get out of this house."

"June, wait, we can't leave—" He caught her arm.

June broke free, a surge of rage flashing through her. "This house is nothing but death and betrayal. I can't be here!"

She spun and ran, tears blinding her as she raced down the hall. Ray's hand closed on her forearm before she reached the stairs. His grip jerked her around, and she lashed out, slamming his chest with her fist. "Let go of me!"

He grabbed her other arm and held it tightly, pulling her close to him. "June, stop. Stop holding on to the past like this," he said softly. "It'll make you crazy. It's time to let it go."

June froze, her voice dropping to a harsh whisper. "What? What did you say?"

"Let go, June. Let JR go. Please."

She stared at him, her eyes stinging and flooded with tears. The weight on her chest felt as if it would crush her. "I can't."

Ray released her arms and cupped her face with both hands. "Yes, you can. You have to. For yourself." He took a deep breath. "For us."

June's knees buckled and she closed her eyes as she sank. Ray wrapped both arms around her, sitting on the floor and pulling her tight against his chest. June clutched the cloth of his shirt, her fingers digging into his shoulders. The grief she'd fought for so long gushed out of her in deep, racking sobs.

Silently, Ray held her, rocking her gently as the crippling anger eased. Slowly, June became aware of how comforting his strength was, how patiently he held her.

How bizarre this must have seemed to him, this strange anger that had come out of nowhere. But he'd simply held on.

He hadn't let her go.

"He promised he'd never lie to me."

Ray stroked her hair. "So I gathered."

June let out a long sigh, her face still pressed against Ray's chest. "He knew how crucial it was that he never lie, how vital it was to our relationship after everything I'd been through."

"I assume you're not talking about little lies like how you look in that new pair of jeans."

June smiled and looked up at him.

He stroked her cheek. "Ah, there you are."

"No, I'm not talking about the love fibs people tell each other." Her smile faded. "Ray, by the time I met JR, I'd lived an entire lifetime of lies. My father. People on the streets. I'd learned to lie in order to survive. It was such a habit, I lied even when I didn't have to. Ask me if I was going to the store and I'd tell you I was going to the library. JR brought me out of that. Telling the truth became our manifesto. We put it in our wedding vows."

June shifted in Ray's arms but made no attempt to push him away. "I knew he had to keep some things private. He'd simply say, 'I can't tell you.'" She waved her hand toward the nursery. "He said the contents of that box were dangerous and he had to destroy them. I believed him. He lied."

"June, if JR lied to you, he must have had a very good reason."

"Good enough to violate my trust?" June shook her head, but Ray stopped her, bracing her cheek in one hand.

"I meant what I said, June. Let him go. For yourself."

June stilled, her eyes staring into his. "For us."

He nodded, then tilted his head and kissed her.

His lips were soft but firm, and June relaxed against him, the tension in her muscles easing as his arms tightened around her. His kiss moved from her lips to her cheek, then to her hair as she leaned her head on his shoulder.

"You are a remarkable woman, June," he whispered. "In God's eyes. And mine. You need to believe that. With all your heart."

June let out a long, slow exhale. "I do."

"Remember that phrase."

June pushed away from him, laughing. "I hate it when you do that. Make me laugh in the midst of my tears."

His eyes brightened with humor. "You love it."

"I do." Her eyes gleamed. "Oh, wait. There's that phrase again."

They both grinned at that, then June nodded back toward the nursery. "You need to call Jeff."

"Those boxes aren't going anywhere."

June leaned back against his chest, wrapping her arms around him. "Neither am I."

Jeff checked the three items found in the niche, logged them for evidence and transported them back to the Bell County Sheriff's Department. Ray and June followed, after one of Ray's officers arrived to keep an eye on the Victorian. Ray didn't want to take chances with the house. His gut told him it still held too many secrets.

He and June rode to the station in silence, both of them itching to examine the contents of the boxes as soon as Jeff was done fingerprinting them. She held her backpack, the hard drive from David's computer still in her laptop, between her feet. He glanced at her occasionally, but she continued to stare out the passenger window, lost in thought.

When she'd bolted from the nursery, JR's betrayal all over her face, Ray had felt a surge of panic and confusion. In his profession, people lied all the time. He had become jaded, almost expecting it on a daily basis. That a lie from JR would cause this kind of crisis in June had caught him off guard.

Lord, have I become that numb to lying that I expect it of people? That I think it would be no reason to be angry?

They both had lived in a world of lies—she as a child

and he on the job. Yet while he had accepted it as fact that everyone lied, June had made a vow never to do it again. It had been part of her transformation.

Recognition flashed through Ray's mind. *No wonder she'd felt betrayed.* It was as if JR himself had attacked that transformation from the grave.

Ray swung the cruiser into a parking space in front of the converted storefront that made up the main office of the Bell County Sheriff's Department. Ray loved the station, and since Anne's death, it had been more like home than work. He'd buried a lot of grief in his hours here, and it had endeared him to the community. He'd been born in Nashville, spent time in the army and started his profession in Memphis, but Bell County was definitely his home.

He opened the door for June, then guided her through the officer's bullpen to the small conference room at the back of the station, where Gage finished fingerprinting the evidence gathered at the house. The date book, shoe box and black tin box sat in the middle of the table. A box of latex gloves sat nearby, and Ray handed June a pair before snapping on his own.

"Where do you want to start?" Ray asked June.

"I want to know what's in that black box."

They pushed chairs away from the table and stood close to the edge as Ray slid the metal box toward them. Gingerly, Ray thumbed open the latch and pulled up the top. Seven envelopes lay inside, unsealed and neatly stacked on top of each other, numbered one through seven.

"That's convenient," June muttered, as Ray opened the first envelope and slipped out the four folded pages inside.

It was Rosalie Osborne's handwritten will.

June gasped, and a hand flew to her mouth. "Do you think that's real?"

Ray let out a long breath. "We have to assume for the moment it is."

"What's it say?"

Ray turned the creased pages carefully. "She leaves everything, including the house, to the White Hills library."

June grew still. "The house, too."

Ray nodded, then paused and pointed to one line. "Read this."

"'Let it be known that this will stands as my final word, so that no person or institution may profit from my estate.'"

"This lady was very unhappy with someone when she wrote this," Ray said.

"What's in number two?"

The second envelope held only one page, and as they read it, Ray felt his spine stiffen. His murder case had just gotten a whole lot bigger.

June stared up at him. "Rosalie's dead."

He nodded once. "And she knew she was going to die."

"And who was going to kill her."

THIRTEEN

Whoever you are, I pray you are a police officer. If you are, then you probably found this during a search of my house following my death.

I dearly wish this wasn't true, but I can't hide my suspicions any longer. I have no proof of those suspicions except what's in this box, but I plan a confrontation tomorrow night.

Whatever happens, know that I love Hunter. Dearly. Without reserve. None of this could be said to be his fault, yet he has paid a great price. And I cannot fully despise Virginia, even given the hatred she has showered on me. In many ways, she is only trying to protect her cub, to be a good mother. That Virginia's idea of good motherhood runs perpendicular to the rest of the planet is what we'll have to discuss.

Hunter needs help. Medication. If going public with his illness is the only way to ensure he gets it, then that's what I'll have to do. I just hope they both understand.

My lawyer tells me that without proof, my conjecture would constitute slander if told the press. What I have gathered so far could be used to produce that proof, but I have not yet taken that step. I'm hoping Virginia will listen to reason. If she doesn't, I'll do what I have to do.

I am only glad that my father is not here to see this. Or perhaps he should be. I do think he would be proud of his child. His children.

In good faith,
Rosalie Osborne
December 12, 1986

June sat back in her chair. "Does that mean what I think it means?"

"We can't be sure."

"Open the others."

Silently Ray lifted the flaps on the remaining envelopes. Three, four and five contained strands of hair with the roots still attached, but there was no indication who the strands belonged to. Envelope six held a list of names and blood types. As she read it, June felt her fascination growing. "This is a time bomb."

Siegfried Osborne—AB Neg
Montgomery Osborne—AB Neg
Eulis Osborne—AB Neg
Rosalie Osborne—AB Neg
Virginia Bridges—A Pos
Jonathan Bridges—O Pos
Hunter Bridges—AB Neg

"Eulis Osborne was Monty's older brother?" Ray asked.

"Right. The one killed in World War I. Jonathan was Virginia's husband. Ray, there's no way that an O-positive father and an A-positive mother produced an AB-negative son. If Hunter is AB-negative, Jonathan cannot be his father. One of the Osbornes must be."

"Her lawyer was correct about slander."

"This isn't slander. Blood types are a matter of fact."

"This could be entirely made up. She says that she loved Hunter. Maybe she begged him to run away with her and he refused. Maybe she left on her own, without going back to her house."

"Leaving everything she loved, not even a suitcase packed? Ray, Rosalie is saying that Hunter Bridges is actually an Osborne. Monty Osborne's son. She was in love with her half-brother. She's also saying that Hunter has a mental illness. Which he inherited from her father."

Ray turned suddenly toward June, his face a hard mask. "This cannot leave this room. Cannot."

She leaned back from him, startled. "Of course not." Her surprise increased as Ray's cheeks paled. "Ray, what's wrong?"

He stood up abruptly, shoving the chair backward. "Stay here. Don't touch anything. I'll be right back."

As the door swung shut behind him, she followed slowly, pausing at the windowed door to watch Ray as he strode across the bullpen, motioning for Jeff Gage to follow him. Then they both disappeared into Ray's office.

"What in the world?" June glanced back at the items on the table, then out over the bullpen again, where several officers stared curiously at Ray's office door. Ray reappeared a moment later, headed back in her direction. June returned to her seat.

Ray closed the door firmly and sat slowly, taking a deep breath and placing his palms flat on the table. "We cannot, under any circumstances, make assumptions about what this means."

"Even though Rosalie did?"

"Yes. She could have been quite wrong with her suppositions."

June peered closer at Ray's stony face. His jaw hardened and his eyes stared at the tin box, making June wonder what turmoil raged behind the mask.

Her voice turned gentle. "Let's see what's in the seventh envelope."

Ray reached for the yellowed envelope, his movements efficient and precise. From it he pulled a business card, a creased and brittle newspaper clipping and a folded eight-by-ten photograph. He put them on the table in front of them, turning over the business card first.

June's throat suddenly felt raw, and she made a sound that fell somewhere between a choke and a cough. "This is not good."

The card said, "Gerald R. Fowler, M.D., Psychiatric Genetic Counselor."

Ray shook his head. "No, it's not." His brow still

furrowed in thought, he gingerly opened the photo, which showed a young blonde woman, tall and elegantly dressed, standing next to a gray-haired man in a wheelchair. Her puffy hairstyle placed the photo in the mideighties.

"Rosalie and Monty, I presume. He would have been close to eighty by the time she came back home."

Ray pulled a pen from his pocket and used it to point out small circles someone had drawn around the man's eyes and brows, his chin and one ear. "What do you think this is about?"

June shrugged. "What's the clipping?"

Using one finger and the tip of his pen, Ray unfolded the newspaper. It was a promotional profile of a young Hunter Bridges, who had been accepted into Vanderbilt University's Law School after having finished his undergraduate studies by the age of twenty. The same circles had been drawn around Hunter's eyes and brows.

"That does make it clear she thought Hunter was Montgomery Osborne's son."

"And probably susceptible to Monty's inherited mental issues." Ray leaned back in his chair, staring at the business card again. "In 1986, DNA testing had barely gotten off the ground. The first conviction because of it wasn't until a year later. Blood tests to establish paternity were available, but Rosalie would have been pushing the edge to use hair samples."

"Which may be why she planned to confront Virginia." June sat straighter in her chair, her stomach tightening painfully. "Ray, I know these two. Virginia has had grand plans for Hunter ever since he was a kid. Accusations of infidelity and mental illness would not be taken lightly. Not in an ambitious family like the Bridges. This is motive."

Ray's stillness grew even more solid and severe. "Motive for what, June? We have no evidence that Rosalie is dead, and if Hunter inherited mental illness from Montgomery Osborne, he obviously has it under control. He graduated from Vanderbilt Law and was in private practice for several years. He's been an elected politician most of his life." He twisted in his chair to face her more directly.

"You've been on the streets. You know what it's like to be around an untreated paranoid schizophrenic. They aren't usually violent. They're chaotic. When they talk, they don't make sense. If they're on medication and stay monitored, however, they can live fairly normal lives. Get married. Hold a job. Maybe even be a lawyer."

"How do you know so much about this?"

Ray hesitated, then plunged back in. "It's part of my job. If I have to confront someone who's agitated, I have to be able to reasonably assess what's going on. We have no proof Rosalie ever confronted Virginia about getting Hunter help, as she said in her letter, and no proof that Hunter or Virginia knows anything about what's in this box. And if they don't know, they'd have no reason to hire Stephen Webster to kill David."

"But she said she was going to confront Virginia!"

"The next night. We don't know that she did."

"How can you be sure?"

"Because Rosalie Osborne disappeared the night she wrote that note. December 12, 1986, is the night Rosalie called the sheriff's department, then vanished into thin air."

Ray watched Daniel Rivers escort June out of the station, knowing exactly how angry she was at him. When he'd refused to pursue the Bridges family mystery, she'd launched from her chair like a rocket, virtually accusing him of playing favorites with the county's number-one son.

Ironic, since some of his own deputies thought he was playing favorites with *her* on this case.

Ray released a long, deep breath as the station door closed behind them. Truth was, he didn't like Hunter any more than she did, but Ray believed in sticking to the facts.

"A case is not about beliefs, June," he said as his office door closed behind him and he dropped into the chair behind his desk. "Hunches may guide you, but in the end, it's about evidence."

And for now, they had little. The items in the tin box proved only that Rosalie had some explosive suspicions. The shoe box held old family photos of the Osbornes, and JR's date book had turned up nothing suspicious, either. Both appeared to be in the niche with the tin box only by coincidence.

He wanted to interview Virginia Bridges, but instinct told him to wait. The only link actually connecting her to this case was a car reported stolen before Webster had tried to kill June with it. If he so much as called her, he knew Virginia would circle an entire wagon train of lawyers around her and Hunter before he could get the words out of his mouth.

No, better to wait on that one until something else turned up. The Bridges were not going anywhere.

Ray scowled. The right decision, yes, but more than forty-eight hours had passed since David Gallagher's death, and the leads were growing colder. Webster remained silent, a good defense attorney already at his side.

But what about Gerald Fowler?

Ray turned to his computer, a quick internet search turning up Fowler's obituary. The doctor had died in 1996, leaving behind a mountain of important DNA research. But even if his patient files still existed in some hospital storage room somewhere, they were still protected by privilege, and Ray didn't have enough probable cause for a warrant.

Ray searched for known associates of Dr. Fowler but turned up little before a sharp knock on his door interrupted him.

"Come!"

Jeff Gage entered and closed the door behind him. The lanky officer sat, his spine stiff and his face solemn.

"I take it you don't have good news."

Gage's lips thinned to a bare line. "Depends on how you define *good*."

Ray leaned forward, bracing his forearms on his desk. "Tell me what you found out about Carter."

Gage cleared his throat. "Okay, but first, the cadaver dog will be here tomorrow morning. Where do you want her to search?"

"That tunnel, then the basement and the grounds around the house."

"You really think Rosalie Osborne is there?"

"With what we found today, I doubt she ever left the house."

"Did you tell June that?"

Ray shook his head. "No. June's already wound tight as a drum about this and involved up to her neck. I need to keep the next few steps in the investigation quieter, if only to protect her."

"Where is she now?"

"I sent her with Daniel. She needs to replace her driver's license and bank card. He'll take her home. Then I'll be on watch at her house until midnight."

"Want me to take over after that?"

"If you're up to it."

"Well, you certainly don't want Carter to do it."

Ray leaned back in his chair and closed his eyes a moment, the disquiet that had been growing in his stomach spreading into his chest.

"Long version or quick and dirty?" Gage asked.

Ray opened his eyes again. "How about somewhere in between?"

Gage nodded once. "You were right, Ray. Brent Carter's blood type is AB-negative. And all those courthouse records are quite informative. You have to go way up the family tree then come down on the other side, but, yep, Brent is kin to the both the Osborne and Bridges clans, on his mother's side. Seems like old Siegfried's first son, Eulis, fathered a child before he was killed. Mother and son left the Osbornes after his death and that son married an ancestor of the Bridges. Brent and Hunter are third or fourth cousins, depending on how you count it. Close enough to garner an invitation to family reunions but not enough to be in any of the wills."

"Close enough to choose blood over your career?"

Gage lifted one shoulder in a half-hearted shrug. "That would depend on the family. I got a whole slew of cousins I wouldn't call to give the time of day. How did you know about Carter's blood type? How did you remember that?"

"A couple of years ago, he went to give blood for a relative. Mentioned that they had a rare blood type. You got the phone records?"

"Came in this morning. They're locked in my trunk."

"Show anything?"

Gage gave another swift nod. "Two calls that morning look as if they are connected to the case. The station records show a call from a prepaid cell the morning of David's murder."

"Any indication which officer took the call?"

"No, sir. It came in just before the 911 call was received. Carter's cell received the second call from the same phone right after the call to 911. Both lasted about two minutes."

"Do we know yet who made the 911 call?"

Gage's expression darkened. "The 911 call came from the same prepaid cell. A woman. Later, just before you and June left for the hospital, a call went out from Brent's cell phone to that same number."

"Virginia."

"That's my guess."

"So Virginia hears the Corvette and recognizes the sound. She flees, calling 911, leaving Webster in the study. Virginia knows we'll find June standing over David's body, which will make us doubt any story she has about seeing anyone else at the scene."

"And the second call to Carter warned him that the plan had gone off base because of June." Jeff took a deep breath. "It gets worse. While we were at the scene, Brent made a call to a different anonymous cell."

"Webster."

Jeff nodded. "He called Webster to tell him what route you were taking to the hospital."

The two men stared at each other as they fought to maintain control in light of the betrayal. The flood of anger washing over Ray made every muscle tense and he could see in Gage's stony expression the same struggle. "Any proof beyond the record of the calls about any of this?"

"No, sir."

Ray stood abruptly, and Gage followed suit. "Bring Carter in here. I want this cleared up now."

"Yes, sir." Gage turned sharply and left the office.

Alone, Ray closed his eyes and allowed himself a moment of pure rage, his fists clenching and unclenching at his sides. Since Webster had first fired at them from that ridge, Ray had known something screwy was going on. Webster had been one step ahead of them all the way. He'd known where June was, and he'd known when the time came to dump the SUV.

But in the back of his mind, Ray had convinced himself that maybe the phones were tapped or someone local was watching them. He'd not wanted to believe the obvious and most likely choice—that it was one of his own men.

Carter. A local kid who'd been one of his most reliable officers for the past few years. Efficient and extremely good at his job. *I guess blood is thicker after all.*

Ray took two deep breaths. The office door popped open again, and Gage's face had gone a shade paler. "Carter's gone. He asked where Daniel was taking June and left right after."

"Get Rivers on his radio."

Gage shook his head. "Dispatch is trying. Radio and cell. He's not responding."

FOURTEEN

June's head throbbed, and she fought the urge to lash out at everything around her. She squeezed her eyes shut. Tears of pure, burning anger slid down her face as she shivered from the overwhelming wrath.

Get it under control! You can't help anyone like this!

Not that she could even help herself at the moment. The trunk of a car wasn't an easy place to escape from. She'd already tried the emergency release latch—disabled. And kicking at the brake lights had only hurt her toes: they were covered with a thick wire mesh.

June made herself take a long, slow breath. Then another. Slowly, her mind cleared as she replayed what had happened. She and Daniel had returned to her cottage after getting her new driver's license and bank card. Daniel had gotten out of the car and checked her house, signaling that all was clear. She'd grabbed the backpack and gotten out, just as an older sedan had pulled up behind Daniel's cruiser. Brent Carter had emerged, motioning for Daniel to come talk to him.

She could still see Daniel greet Carter with the openness and welcome of a fellow officer. Then his face twisted with the shock of betrayal as Carter shoved a Taser into Daniel's chest. Daniel had dropped heavily, shuddering, against the fender of his own cruiser, then to the ground.

June ground her teeth, angry at herself for not reacting quicker. When Daniel fell, June tried to run, stumbling, digging in her pocket for her cell phone. Carter had been faster, grabbing her from behind and batting the phone away. He'd knocked her to the ground with a single blow. She'd been stunned and woozy when he'd picked her up, backpack still clutched in her hands, and tossed her into the trunk of the waiting car.

Carter. One of Ray's own men. He'd been one of her guards, had been at the Victorian when…

When my car exploded.

A numbing calm settled over June as realization set in. Carter had been on his own at the parsonage the day before. He'd left the scene of David's murder to clear the crowd away from the house. With all the time in the world to call Webster and tell him the route Ray planned to take to the hospital.

June squeezed her eyes shut tighter, her balled fists pressing into her stomach. She had to get out of this. Ray would never suspect Carter. She had to find a way to get out—

The car picked up speed suddenly, pitching June toward the back. In the distance, she could hear the

distinctive sound of a train's horn and the bells of a
crossing.

He's trying to beat a train across the tracks!

"Are you insane?" June shouted, even though she
knew he couldn't hear her. "What are you doing?"
Almost out of instinct, she banged on the trunk. "Stop!
Have you lost your mind?"

The roar of the train's diesel engine joined the horn,
echoing around the trunk as if it were on top of the car.
The car's brakes and tires abruptly screeched in tandem,
and June hurtled toward the front of the car, banging
her head, ribs and shins against the spare tire and an
assortment of metal objects that rocketed around the
trunk.

Her fury exploded as she screamed from the pain and
pummeled her fists on the trunk's roof. She felt the metal
give under her wrath, popping small dents outward. As
the train's sounds faded, June's rage became words. "Let
me out of here! Ray Taylor will rip out your spine, you
traitorous—"

The car jackrabbited forwarded again, spinning one
wheel and sending the smell of burning rubber flooding
into the trunk. June's cries broke off into yelps as the
car bounced twice, leveled off, then bounced again.

June clamped her mouth shut, her mind racing.
Bounce. Level. Bounce. Level. An image snapped into
her mind. Only one railroad crossing in Bell County
had that peculiar space between double tracks. Simpson
Pike, the road that led straight from White Hills into
Kentucky's Simpson County.

He's taking me out of state.

And out of Ray Taylor's jurisdiction.

"Oh, no, you don't." June's thoughts clicked through the businesses along Simpson Pike as she twisted, her hands searching the trunk for the backpack. She found it near her feet and clawed it open, pulling out her laptop. She opened it and booted it up, the bright light from the screen almost blinding her in the pitch-black of the trunk.

About two miles north of the railroad crossing, two strip malls had sprung up on a crossroads that connected several new subdivisions with the interstate. One of the most popular businesses was a coffee shop offering live music at night, its own special blends of fourteen different coffees…and free Wi-Fi. She watched the laptop move through its start-up routine, praying fervently that the coffee shop sat close enough the road…and that the stoplight would turn red as they approached.

Daniel River's fist hit the hood of his cruiser hard enough to leave a dent, and the abrupt, hollow thud made more than one officer take a step away from the deputy, who still leaned heavily against the fender, fighting to remain standing.

Ray stood his ground. "He gave you no reason to be suspicious, Rivers."

Daniel shook his head, more in disgust at himself than in acknowledgment of Ray's statement. "He wasn't in uniform. And he was driving that trashed old sedan of his mother's. I should have known something was up."

"Did he say anything?"

Another shake of the head. "Not really. I was up toward the house, and he motioned for me. Said he had a message from you. Then he punched me with the Taser."

"Did you go out?"

"No. June tried to run, but he caught her, knocked her down. I found her phone in the yard. She tried to call 911."

"Was she unconscious?"

"Stunned. She'd started to fight by the time he dumped her in the trunk."

"I pulled the license plate when I got your call and alerted the Tennessee Highway Patrol as well as all our guys. I want everyone on cell phones, in case Carter has a scanner." Ray took a deep, bracing inhale, one of his best weapons in his war to stay calm and focused on finding June. A lot of years had passed since he'd felt this kind of deep, searing panic in his gut.

Daniel straightened, squaring his shoulders. "Are we going to his place?"

"I'd already dispatched Gage to Carter's house when we got the 911 call from June's neighbors." Ray explained how he'd just learned about Carter's family connections to the Bridges.

"We can't just wait here!"

"We're not. Martha's pulling records on any property Carter or his parents own. I'll call her when you're ready to ride."

"Let's go."

Ray pulled the cell phone from his belt and called the Bell County sheriff's dispatcher. Martha Williams had been on their phones for almost thirty years and often conducted background research for their officers. When she answered, Martha's words spilled out like an excited teenager.

"Ray! I was just about to call you. We just got the weirdest 911 call on the planet. It has to be June."

Ray's eyebrows arched, and he held up a hand, motioning Daniel to wait. "Tell me."

"Emerson Pitt called in. He had some day workers in his pickup, taking them over to his place, when they had to stop for a train."

"Get to it, Martha."

"An old sedan tried to beat the train and wound up hitting the brakes instead. Slid right in next to Emerson's truck. His workers got all excited after the train passed. They claim they heard someone banging inside the car's trunk, screaming."

Ray yanked open his cruiser door and got in, pulling back on the road before Daniel could get the passenger door closed. It slammed as Ray gunned the big engine and the car leaped forward. "Where?"

"Simpson Pike. The double crossing."

"Headed for Kentucky."

"Looks like."

"Expand that search, Martha. Include any property owned by Virginia or Hunter Bridges as well."

The dispatcher hesitated. "You're sure?"

"Do it, Martha."

"On it, Ray."

Ray flipped the phone closed, then slung the cruiser into a tight turn north.

June braced the laptop in the crook of her arm and typed out a message with one finger. She'd pulled her feet up and braced her knees against the spare tire, her back against the rear of the trunk, in an effort to remain as stable as possible. Sharp corners and edges of metal dug into her skin with every bounce and bump.

She kept one eye on her Wi-Fi status, knowing her window of opportunity was minuscule at best. She prayed that Carter would stick to the speed limit, which was twenty-five through the crossroads.

"First time I've ever been grateful for a speed trap," she muttered as the car slowed. A low beep indicated that her link to the café's server was hot, and she logged in as the car came to a halt, idling roughly. She clicked Send, then held her breath as the car accelerated again.

The link disappeared, the connection lost. No confirming message or beep.

June fought back disappointment that bordered on despair. Maybe it went. Maybe they'd be looking anyway.

Please, Lord?

She activated the GPS tracker she'd installed in the laptop just after she'd bought it, closed the lid and pushed the computer back into the backpack. Uncurling and trying to ease the pressure on her back, June felt around the spare tire until she found a space big enough for the backpack. Maybe when he let her out, he wouldn't remember he'd put the backpack in here with her.

If he let her out.

FIFTEEN

Just past the crossroads, the car turned left off Simpson Pike and began a circuitous route through the backcountry of northern Tennessee and southern Kentucky. For the next hour or so, June focused on prayer and whatever sounds she could hear. She kept expecting fear to rush in and cloud her mind, but it never did. The anger hovered, keeping her stomach tense, but the more she prayed, the more calm she found herself.

Even though she knew that she might die.

June turned this over in her mind a few times. Dying had ceased to frighten her years ago, the moment she realized her brother, Marc, was gone. She'd stared at him for a long time after their father had savagely beaten him, strangely relieved that his pain had finally ended. He was at peace. Now, after her years with JR and a newfound faith, she knew Marc was with God. Back then she just knew her father could no longer inflict pain on her beloved brother.

Back then death just brought release. Now it meant being with her Lord.

No, the idea of death held no fear. But lying there in the dark, unaware of what even the next hour would bring, June realized that all her rage, her despair, came from the possibility of losing Ray.

It was his face that kept appearing in her mind, and a desire to hold him settled over June, as crystal clear an emotion as she had felt in a long time. "Lord," she whispered, "I've never felt anything like this. You get me out of this, and I'll never walk away from that man again."

The car turned right but June had lost all sense of whether they had turned north, south, east or west. The back roads of this part of the country meandered, and a driver could easily start out heading west and wind up heading northeast before reaching a destination.

June still felt amazed by Brent's actions. Tall and bulky, still single in his forties, Brent Carter had been an active member of her own church. He'd been with the sheriff's department for more than a decade. What drove him to do something like this?

Money? Maybe, but it would have to be part of something else, something bigger.

Blood kin? June felt her senses perk up a bit. That would do it. People could always be tempted by money, but in these parts, blood held a deeper sway. Brent had been loyal to his parents until their deaths. She remembered him bringing his mother to church, even when she couldn't walk anymore. He'd pick her up and carry her in, if he had to.

June had known men like that all her life. *Stay calm,*

girl. If you attack him, he'll sulk up. You'll need to talk your way out of this one.

She groaned as the car slowed almost to a stop, then bounced hard over what felt like a cattle grate in a driveway. The car proceeded slowly, then the sound changed entirely, shifting from the echo of open space to the flat noise of enclosure. She heard a garage door descending and squinted, preparing for the return of light.

The trunk latch popped, and the lid rose gradually. June lay still and opened her eyes slowly. She made no attempt to lunge at her attacker—not that it would have done any good, given that he held a 9 mm pistol in his left hand.

She cleared her throat. "Awfully long way to come for a murder."

Brent, who had sat on the right side of the White Hills Gospel Immanuel Chapel for most of his life, grimaced. "No killing. Not yet anyway."

"Stephen Webster certainly seemed determined to kill me."

Brent snorted. "Webster was an idiot. A huge, out-of-control mistake. We were about to take care of that when Ray did it for us."

"You're feeling awfully chatty today."

"Like it matters if I am or not. Get out of the trunk, June. Don't act like you don't know what's going on."

He stepped back, and June grabbed the edge of the trunk to pull herself up. "I'm stiff. That's not exactly a comfortable place to ride." She struggled to find a flat place to brace her knee and swing her leg out. Brent reached out and grabbed the back of her jeans, hauling her out of the car and holding on until she found her feet.

"If I thought for a second you'd keep that mouth of yours shut, you could have ridden up front."

"Not exactly something I'm known for."

"No. Walk through the door on the right. And I *will* shoot you if you get out of hand. Not to kill you. Just someplace where it'll really hurt."

"I've been shot before, Brent. It hurts, no matter where."

He chuckled, but the sound held little humor. "Oh, right. You're the pastor's wife with the criminal past."

"And for the record, I do *not* know what's going on."

"That I doubt."

June looked around at Brent, then at the garage itself. A two-car structure, but only the space where Brent's car sat had an opener attached to the door. The other could be opened with its latch. Handy. "It's true. And this is the cleanest garage I've ever seen."

"Stop casing the place. You won't have a chance to run."

"And my guess is we're a far piece from a main road."

"A piece, yes."

June reached for the doorknob and let herself into the huge kitchen of a pristine country home. The spotless tile floor matched, in both design and color, the granite countertops. The glass-front cabinets revealed high-end china and crystal. Even the pots hanging from a rack over a center island looked as if they cost a fortune. Spotless, but with the clinging scent of a long-unused and closed house. "Hunter's summer palace, perhaps? Or Virginia's?"

"And you said you didn't know what was going on."

June stopped, turning to face him. "I really don't. Suspicions, but no facts."

"Virginia's. Comes here to get away from the hustle and bustle of her law firm, so she says."

"And her king making?"

"She does have plans for Hunter, that's for sure." He motioned with the gun. "Den's through there."

June pushed through a swinging door and stepped down into a room steeped in amber-tinted stone and burgundy leather. A six-foot-wide fireplace sat in a hearth on the far side of the room, and the heavy chairs and couch looked more suited to large men back from a hunt, not a petite lawyer who didn't quite reach June's own short height. "This must be Hunter's space when he's here."

"His and his boys. There's a big high-definition television behind that painting."

"Clever. Could be a fun room."

"You won't be here that long. We're just waiting. We had to get you out of town long enough to plan the next move. This place would be too easy for Ray to find. If you know this is about Hunter and Virginia, he does, too."

"Mother and son," June muttered. "You ever see *The Manchurian Candidate?*"

Brent laughed and motioned for her to sit on a stool in the middle of the room. "Sit there. So what is it that you have against Hunter, anyway? You think he has some kind of little time bomb in his head? Some programming that'll go haywire once he's in the state senate?"

June perched on the stool, watching Brent closely as she said her next few words in a low, even voice. "Oh, I think we both know he does. A big one. They don't want people knowing, and they don't like loose ends. That's why they killed Rosalie Osborne. Why they killed David. Why they'll kill me. And you."

June could see Brent's struggle to keep his face impassive. The muscles in his cheeks tightened, and the skin beneath his dark eyes paled. His lips thinned and grew white as he pressed them together, resisting her words.

June pressed her advantage, calling on every ounce of her imagination. She kept her voice soft, hushed, as she spun the tale she'd dwelled on while in Brent's trunk. "Virginia must have been a sweet kid back in the day. Beautiful. Innocent. Her husband was older, gone a lot. She was lonely. Then she met Monty. He lured her in. Preyed on her naïveté. Everyone knew what he was like, right?"

Brent stood still, watching her, listening, his eyelids slightly lowered.

"She just thought he liked her company. She wasn't the first. She wasn't the last. No one knew the baby she delivered belonged to Monty. Until Rosalie fell in love with Hunter. Then Virginia tried to stop them. They resented it. Maybe they decided to elope, went to get the blood test for a license—"

"No." Brent's flat voice covered any emotion in his words. "They gave blood. The Red Cross puts your blood type on the donor cards. Hunter noticed his blood type didn't match his mother or father. Rosalie noticed it matched hers and her father's. She put it together."

"You're friends with Hunter?"

"Cousins. He's a few years older. Was always the cool kid at family reunions. We followed him around like he was God." Brent shrugged off the spell of the story and sat on the arm of one of the overstuffed leather chairs.

"So he knew his mom had cheated on his dad."

Brent nodded. "Talked about it as if it made his mom sophisticated. We were teenage boys. We thought it was some big adventure, like having a secret identity, or a spy in the family."

"Until Hunter started to get sick and Rosalie threatened to expose what had happened. None of that fit in with Virginia's plans for the future."

Brent shook his head. "Rosalie Osborne was just a cruel woman who thought of no one but herself. She broke Hunter's heart. She ran away and left everyone who cared about her."

"Brent, Rosalie Osborne was the daughter of a paranoid schizophrenic. A disease often passed from father to son. Hunter could be dangerous."

Brent stood slowly, wearily. "You don't think I know that?"

June stared at him. "You know?"

He shrugged and tucked the gun in the waistband of his jeans. "Of course I know."

June stood up, the realization of how deeply Brent was involved dawning on her. "You get the meds for him."

"Every month. His dad got the meds illegally while he was alive. After he died, they came to me. For his career, they said. Cops have access to all sorts of things on the black market. It's always been pretty simple."

"How did David come into the picture?"

"He grew a conscience." Brent went to the window and opened the curtains, revealing a beautiful, expansive lake, the centerpiece of the property. "Man, I hate secrets. This family is eaten up by them. Life would be so much easier if people would just tell the truth."

"It's harder for some."

Brent sniffed. "You got that right." He turned to her again. "About a year ago, Pastor Gallagher found something in the parsonage that revealed everything. He went to Hunter, but Hunter persuaded his own pastor to keep quiet. Promised to stay on the meds and gave the church a big donation."

"But he didn't stay on the meds."

Brent gave a low laugh of derision. "Hunter has more ego than two or three men. He goes off, goes back on, stops."

"And David saw the cycle."

Brent nodded. "Finally. Realized Hunter had manipulated him into silence like he did everyone. David told Hunter he'd broken a trust."

"And Hunter had him killed."

"Virginia. She knew about Webster from some of her dealings on a case in Florida. She made that call."

"What about Kitty?"

"Webster. He did it when she wouldn't tell where David hid the evidence. He and I put the body in the house before Daniel got there."

"Why are you telling me all this?"

Brent shrugged again, and a deep veil of sadness fell over his face. "This is my last task for Hunter. He called in a marker I had to repay, even though it will take everything from me." His face grew even darker. "Everything, June. This time helping him meant giving up everything."

June shook her head, a touch of desperation for this sad man tightening her stomach. "Brent, no. Ray will work with you on any charges against you. Hunter and Virginia are responsible. The proof is still in that house somewhere."

"And that," came a dark baritone voice from behind June, "is the only reason why *you* are still alive."

"This is killing me." Daniel crossed his arms over his chest and planted his feet wide. "We should be chasing them down. *Doing* something."

The corner of Ray's mouth twitched, but otherwise he remained still, staring at the back wall of Virginia

Bridges's summer home. He knew exactly how his chief deputy felt. Inside, he felt as if he were being clawed apart by the raw power of his emotions, but he didn't dare release a single ounce of it.

Daniel shifted his weight from one foot to the other. "At least this removes any doubt about the Bridgeses' involvement."

"Plausible deniability. This is Virginia's vacation home. Not a residence. They have a caretaker and a maid who come in regularly. The family is only here irregularly. They can claim someone broke in, raise reasonable doubt."

They stood, waiting on a warrant to be delivered by the local Kentucky sheriff. The garage door stood wide open, revealing empty space, and the windows showed no signs of activity. The GPS signal from June's laptop had vanished less than ten minutes before they arrived, removing any last bit of probable cause they had for entering the house.

Ray flipped open his cell phone again and called Gage, who monitored the computer tracking system from the station. "Any change?"

"Not yet." Gage's voice held the same stress they all felt. "Anything there?"

"Still waiting on the warrant. Call me if you get anything."

"Will do."

Ray flipped the phone shut, frustration building to a boiling point. Abruptly, he started toward the house.

"Ray?"

"I'm not waiting. The warrant will be here."

"You said—"

"I'm not waiting." Ray's boots echoed loudly in the empty garage, and he drew his gun, holding it down to one side as he peered through the rectangular windows of the kitchen door. Testing the knob, he found it unlocked and pushed the door open, swiveling around the frame, gun at the ready. Daniel came in behind him, following protocol. They cleared each room, finding only an abandoned house that looked more like a museum than a home.

Until they came to the den. June's laptop lay in the center of the floor, smashed almost beyond recognition. "This explains why we lost the signal. They took the hard drive."

"Sir?"

Ray turned to find Daniel staring down at one of the burgundy leather chairs. "What did you find?"

Daniel looked up at him. "Blood. This chair is covered in blood."

"Ray Taylor was and always will be a Marine. That makes him deadly and efficient but also predictable. He'll follow the rules. He'll wait for a warrant and the outcome of evidence. Unless he has a body, he won't step outside the boundaries. It's just who he is."

Hunter's rambling and sometimes nonsensical monologue had continued for thirty minutes, and June found her rage returning in full force. Only the duct tape on her mouth kept her silent—she'd learned quickly that struggling against it hurt like crazy. Hunter's useless and self-serving prattle made her nuts. If she could have freed her wrists and ankles from the plastic ties that bound them, she would have launched up off the back-seat and gladly throttled him.

"That's the difference between someone who makes laws and someone who enforces them. Politicians, we have more freedom, and since we know how the laws are made, we know how to best use them to our own advantage. It makes everything run a lot smoother."

June felt the huge SUV swerve to the left, and a tall shadow passed over the right side of the vehicle. June looked up. A truck?

A second shadow passed, as June tuned out Hunter's meandering speech.

A convoy, maybe? She knew they couldn't see into the SUV through the tinted windows, but maybe Hunter had overlooked something…like the locks on the back doors.

June dropped her feet over the edge of the seat, catching her heel at the front and pulling back. The shoe on her right foot slid off, and she scooted closer to the passenger side of the SUV. Raising her legs, she curled her toes around the door handle.

Behind her back, June searched with her fingers for the seat belt latch as she waited for the next truck. She wanted to send a signal, not slide out into the road, so she grasped the seat belt with both fists, holding on tightly as another shadow started over the SUV.

June curled her toes and pulled. The door popped

open, almost slamming shut again from the wind. She kicked out hard once, then twice as the door flew open and tried to slam shut. Each time the door whipped back and forth, she slid closer to the opening. Her grip on the seat belt slipped, and she felt a fingernail rip as she tried desperately to hang on.

Hunter let out a barrage of curses and slammed on the brakes, skidding out into the median. The force flung June to the floor with a thud that sent rockets of pain into her left hip. The back door slashed open so hard she heard the hinges pop. She twisted onto her back, trying to get her legs out the door, and curled around the bottom of the car. That could give her enough leverage to pull herself out and to the ground. She couldn't run, but he'd have to pick her up to get her back in the vehicle. Maybe someone would see. The longer she struggled with the door open, the better the chance that someone would see, would call 911.

Please, God.

Twisting over the front seat, Hunter reached down, grabbing her by the shoulder and belt, trying to yank her legs back into the car. June kicked out in an attempt to fling herself out the door. They struggled furiously, June slipping ever so close to the edge.

Suddenly, Hunter released her shoulder, and June realized too late why. She barely registered that his hand had closed into a fist before it slammed into the side of her face, and her world sank into an unrelenting darkness.

SIXTEEN

They found Brent Carter in his car, submerged eight feet below the surface of the grand lake that came almost up to the front door of the Bridgeses' vacation home. When the local sheriff had arrived with a warrant and a crime scene unit, one of the officers had gotten suspicious about an odd set of tire tracks in the yard and had dived in to take a look.

Ray, arms crossed over his chest, stared out over the surface of the placid lake. Daniel satisfied his need to do something by acting as liaison with the local team, relaying messages as the crime-scene officers went over the house with a fine-tooth comb. Ray had ordered that Virginia Bridges be brought into the station for questioning and had sent Gage to a judge for a warrant for the arrest of Hunter Bridges. Plausible deniability was one thing; blood spatter and a dead officer was something else entirely.

To Ray's left, a coroner's van backed slowly toward the lake, and a tow truck arrived to begin the retrieval of Brent's car. They both waited, engines idling, as the

Kentucky officers continued processing the scene. Ray tried to push away memories of working with Brent Carter, of how close they'd been as colleagues and friends. It was hard to believe Brent had betrayed him, but harder still to believe he was gone.

Daniel came up on his right and both watched for a moment as a diver went into the water with a cable. "Why do you think Hunter did it?"

"You ever been around a paranoid schizophrenic off his meds?"

"No."

"This is an illness that most people don't understand and has been badly portrayed in the media. If it's well managed, you might never know someone had it. Just like no one realized that Hunter Bridges had it. He's almost fifty. Finished law school and practiced. Successful man. Elected to various offices. Probably because Rosalie did, in fact, confront Virginia to tell her. Virginia took charge, got Hunter help. But she couldn't leave Rosalie out there knowing that secret. The Bridges ambition cost Rosalie her life."

"So you do think she's dead."

Ray nodded once. "I think June called that one. And if Rosalie loved Hunter enough to step out on that limb, I suspect Hunter loved her as well. He's never married. And I know he liked David Gallagher and relied on his counsel."

"So you don't think he had anything to do with their deaths?" Daniel asked.

"No. But I think he recently found out his mother did.

It's pushed him toward the edge." Ray nodded toward the lake. "People who manage an illness this serious build walls to protect themselves. They have to. They keep loved ones close and anyone untrustworthy out of range. Virginia Bridges has been Hunter's fortress his whole life. If he's found out his mother killed the only woman he ever loved, all those walls could crumble. He's off his meds and spiraling. We have to find June. And soon."

Daniel hesitated. "How do you know—?"

"Anne. It's the real reason we never had kids."

Both men fell silent a few moments, then Ray's cell rang. He snapped it open.

"Boss, we may have something." Ray's face hardened as he listened to Martha Williams describe the 911 call she'd received only moments before. "A trucker, headed south on I-65. Said he saw a man and a woman struggling in a big SUV. He thought it looked like she was tied up, but she was putting up too much of a fight for him to be sure. Got so bad they ran off the road, but he's pretty sure the SUV passed him later, moving lickety-split. Maybe ninety or more. Exited off 117."

"Hunter Bridges own a black SUV?"

"A big one. A Navigator." She rattled off the license plate number.

Ray hung up and looked at Daniel. "They're headed back to White Hills."

Daniel's eyes brightened. "Now we chase him down?"

Ray turned and headed for his cruiser. "Now we chase him down."

* * *

June awoke to the repeated snapping of metal against metal. The heavy odors of gun oil, old wood and dust filled her nose, and she fought back a sneeze as she opened her eyes. Only a few feet away, Hunter Bridges sat in a straight-backed wooden chair, staring out one of the small windows that lined the attic of the Victorian parsonage. Silhouetted by the golden light of late afternoon and haloed by dust drifting in the sun's rays, Hunter sat with his shoulders hunched. In his right hand, he clutched Brent Carter's 9 mm automatic, repeatedly releasing the magazine from its grip, catching it and snapping it back into place. The gun he'd used to kill Brent.

June moved slightly, stretching out her legs, only to be hit by soreness that seemed to hold every muscle in check. She groaned, realizing that the tape on her mouth had been removed, as had the plastic ties around her ankles and wrists.

Hunter stilled, clutching the gun in both hands. "My mother killed Rosalie Osborne."

June licked her lips, then cleared her throat. "I know."

Hunter nodded several times, then the right side of his face twitched with a sharp tic. He blinked, rubbing his face vigorously. "You knew about the documents."

June pushed herself into a sitting position, trying not to moan from the pain, "Not until this morning."

His voice turned sharp. "Don't lie!"

June inhaled deeply, startled at how much her ribs

hurt. "I didn't. I think JR knew. And David. But they never told me. JR said he'd destroyed the documents."

Again, the rapid head nods. "JR." He sniffed and rubbed the side of his head again, this time digging his fingers into his hair for a few moments. "Right. He knew." He glanced her way for a second, then back out the window. "He wasn't the man you think he was. You never knew some of the things he did."

A flush of anger flared in June's chest, but she willed it back. Now was not the time to get defensive. "Hunter—"

"He protected you. A lot." He glanced at her again, then away. "He thought you were fragile. I never saw that. Mother, she had you investigated when y'all first got here. I knew what you'd gone through. What you'd survived."

"Everyone has problems in their past."

He grinned, then ran his hand along the barrel of the gun, back and forth. "You and I have a lot in common, June. We survive. Whatever it takes, we survive."

June swallowed hard, her throat still dry and tight. "Is that a bad thing?"

He shook his head. "No. Just makes us different. Not like the others. JR. My mother. They were users. David, too, somewhat, though not so much." He sat straighter and rolled his shoulders. "When David found those papers, he offered to help, just like Brent did—" He stopped, staring down at the gun. "Why did I do that? Why did I shoot—" His voice broke again, and he shook his head vigorously, as if to rid himself of a horrendous thought.

The image of Brent's death flooded June's mind and she fought against panic. Now was not the time. "Hunter—"

"David...David, he just wanted to help. That's what he said. He could watch for signs that the meds were off, make sure that no one else could tell." His face contorted again, a split second of agony. "Nothing in return. Just the trust. JR, on the other hand—" Hunter paused, then turned to face her, abruptly turning the gun on her as if it were a laser pointer.

June gasped, flinching, but Hunter continued, punctuating every other word with the barrel of the gun. "JR, now, he dreamed big. You saw what he'd made of the church, how he made sure it got plenty of publicity, plenty of new building programs."

"What's wrong with—"

Hunter erupted from the chair. "Because he did it with my mother's money!"

June shook her head, struggling hard to keep her anger under control. She pushed up on her knees to gain more height, but she was still afraid to stand. "He wouldn't—"

"He did!" Hunter started to pace, marching around the attic in off-kilter circles, dodging boxes and old furniture. "After he found the papers, my mother increased her donations to the church three times over. It didn't look like a bribe or extortion because it went into the plate."

"Hunter—"

"That's why she killed him, too!"

Ray focused on the road in front of him, and on the handling of the cruiser. The siren and lights cleared traffic out of their way, as cars and trucks shifted right to allow them passage. Ray veered the car off exit 117, heading west and south, and his familiarity with the country roads let him swing the powerful car easily through the tight turns and sharp curves. He cut the siren and the lights well before he hit White Hills, slowing and entering town at almost the posted speed limit.

Daniel, who had been silent the entire trip, spoke evenly. "Are you sure he'll take her to the parsonage?"

"I'm guessing that he thinks the evidence is still there somewhere."

"Do you have a plan?"

"To go in through the tunnel."

Daniel nodded his approval. "That'll put us out directly on the second floor. A flanking maneuver."

"We'll park on the street near the church, and we can enter the garden area near the spring house without being seen from the parsonage." He turned the cruiser down a side street, then eased it into an alley behind the church.

Daniel got out first. "I'll get the vests."

Ray followed, double-checking his flashlight's power, then his gun, as Daniel dug into the trunk. "I'm praying he's not dangerous."

"Counting on a miracle?"

"Almost every day," Ray muttered, reaching for his own bulletproof vest. "I depend on them."

June choked and coughed, her chest and throat tightening as if Hunter had punched her again. "What?"

Hunter kept pacing, making his frantic circles around the attic, staring at the floor in front of his feet. "Mother. You don't mess with Mother's affairs. She's been a lawyer too long. Defense attorney." He poked himself in the chest with the gun. "Me. I'm corporate. A politician. I know other politicians. I know businesspeople. Stab you in the back, sure, but with a fountain pen, their bank accounts, not in the side." He shuddered and clutched the gun in both hands again. "Mother knows men who kill. Have killed. Did kill. David. And JR."

June sank back to a sitting position, her mind going numb. "No."

The hoarse cracking of her voice made Hunter pause, and he looked at her, his eyes shifting from frantic and crazed to sad. He dropped to his knees in front of her, and tears filled his eyes and spilled over, streaming down his cheeks. "I thought you knew."

June shook her head, the numbness spreading through her body as she stared at him. "It was a heart attack," she whispered.

Hunter dropped his voice to match hers. "Mother. She defended a pharmacist accused of poisoning a customer. He got her the drug. It looks like a heart attack. She put it in the water under the pulpit."

June covered her mouth with both hands, shaking her head.

"I was there. I saw him fall."

"Why didn't you stop her?" June whispered through her cupped hands.

"I didn't know until it was over." Hunter's right eye twitched again, and he hit the side of his face twice with the heel of his hand.

"You didn't know?" June dropped her hands away from her mouth, waves of grief and fear washing through her now as tears streamed down her face. "How could you not know?"

He shook his head, and he looked down at the floor, his eyes half-lidded. "She used me, June. Used my position. Used my illness. Used my...I never knew before. Only after. Never before. Not with JR. Or David. Or... or..." Hunter looked up again, staring at her, unable to say the name.

"Or Rosalie."

Hunter jerked back from her, his eyes wide and wild. A ragged, grief-laden scream burst from him, sending a bolt of pure fear through June. She pushed backward and stumbled to her feet, backing into a table. She stared at one of the most tortured men she'd ever met, and an image flashed through her mind: JR in the downtown soup kitchen, how he'd handled men and women suffering from the same mental illness, homeless and desperate on the street. She saw those same people in a cardboard-box village, sitting among piles of old clothes and garbage, staring into nothingness, lost in their own minds. JR walking among them, helping, listening, offering hope.

June took a step forward and commanded him to stop with his name. "Hunter!" The scream stopped, and he hesitated, staring at her. "She lied, Hunter. JR helped people. He didn't hurt them. You told him, didn't you? Told him what was in your head. You trusted him. Like you did Rosalie. They just wanted to help you. Not hurt you. They loved you."

Hunter blinked at her, his brow furrowed as he focused on her words. June realized he was staring at her mouth, so she said it again. "They loved you. They would have helped. Let me help you."

"Do you love me?"

"I love you. God loves you. Let us help you."

Hunter shook his head, clutching the pistol to his chest. "You won't shoot me?"

Confused, June shook her head. "I won't shoot you, Hunter. I don't have a gun."

Hunter's gaze shifted to a spot behind her. "They do."

Ray Taylor stared at the two people in front of him, using his last ounce of will power not to shoot Hunter Bridges.

He and Daniel had heard Hunter's ranting from the second floor and made their way silently to the attic. With every step, the rantings became clearer, and Ray's anger ran deep, down to a place and time that he thought he'd long ago dealt with and moved beyond.

As they entered the attic, he'd heard Hunter use his illness to turn June from an enemy, a captive, into a sympathetic caregiver, wickedly calling on the grief of her loss and the pain of her past to turn her to his side. To the core of his being, Ray knew that he was not listening to a mentally ill man off his medications. Instead, he was hearing a skilled lawyer preparing an insanity defense.

With June as his star witness.

June spun around, her eyes flaring wide as she saw Ray and Daniel, guns aimed and ready. She threw up both hands, palms toward them. "Don't shoot him!"

Ray's throat closed off when he saw June's injuries, and he struggled to maintain his calm...and his aim. Her right eye, swollen and darkened from a hard punch, was the centerpiece of a field of contusions and bruises.

Daniel spoke first, his normal baritone low and gravelly. "Step out of there, June."

June shook her head furiously. "He's sick, Daniel. Ray, can't you see he's sick? He's off his medication! You can't shoot him!"

Behind June, Hunter stepped a bit closer to her, carefully putting her between him and the two officers.

Ray tensed every muscle and held his aim steady. "June, all I ask is that you listen to me like you've never listened to me before."

"Ray—"

"Listen! Think about what Hunter just said to you. *What* he said, not *how* he said it. How logically it progressed to persuade you."

Some of the anxiety and worry drained away from June's expression. Her eyes narrowed, and her jaw became more set.

Good girl. You know where I'm going. "Now think about the people you knew in the street. The ones truly off their meds. How much sense did they make? When they tried to convince you of something, how grounded in reality was it? How organized?"

June opened her mouth to answer, but Hunter reacted quicker, bellowing at her. "Don't listen to him! He wants to kill me!"

Startled, June jolted to one side and tried to turn, but Hunter grabbed her arm and kept her facing the officers. With one hand, he pulled her against his chest, wrapping his other arm around her neck and shoulders, pressing the gun against her shoulder. "He wants to kill me! They all want to kill me! June! Protect me!"

June's eyes widened again, this time in confusion. Ray had to make it clear for her, had to jerk her mind back to him.

"Remember what we said in the conference room? You asked how I knew so much."

Hunter pointed the gun at Ray and Daniel. "Don't listen to him! He's lying!"

"I know so much because of Anne, June. The disease isn't violent. But the person can be."

June's brows arched, and a light of understanding came into her eyes. "Let me go, Hunter. We can walk out of this."

Hunter Bridges's voice changed in a heartbeat, from

raving lunatic to coldblooded killer. "Not in this lifetime, sister. You are my ticket out."

In the next few seconds, Ray was grateful he'd never lowered his weapon, never dropped his guard. He barely registered the coming explosion in June's eyes before she erupted. In a sudden flash of dual action, she shot her elbow backward into Hunter's solar plexus and stamped down on the instep of his foot. He huffed from the pain and his grip on her loosened. June dropped to the floor, falling free and rolling to one side.

And Ray Taylor, former sniper and excellent marksman, pulled the trigger.

SEVENTEEN

June stood, shivering slightly in the night air, watching the EMTs load Hunter into the ambulance. Her entire body ached, and she felt as if every muscle had been pummeled with a rolling pin. She knew the bruises on the left side of her face would get worse before they got better, as would the black eye. Even now, she could barely see out of it.

She could hear fine, however, and as Hunter struggled against the straps on the gurney, he raised his head to glare, heaping a string of promised punishments at her. They stopped only when the ambulance doors slammed. She watched it pull away, her mind still filled with more questions than answers.

Ray walked up behind her, draping a jacket around her shoulders. "I found this in the cruiser."

She tugged it around her, then slipped her arms into the oversized sleeves. "Thank you." She motioned at the receding ambulance. "I thought you were going to kill him."

"No need. You were out of danger. Just needed to disarm and stop him."

June thought about that a second. "You want to see him suffer the humiliation of a trial."

"Me? Never crossed my mind."

June smiled up at him. "Lying is a sin."

He nodded, solemn-faced but with a light in his eyes. "So is taking revenge." He gently touched her right cheek. "Although I admit to being sorely tempted when I saw what he'd done to you."

"It looks worse than it is."

"Hm."

June let out a long, exhausted sigh. "What now?"

"First, we take you to NorthCrest to get checked out."

"Isn't that how this whole adventure got started? I'm really—"

"Don't argue. I heard what you did trying to escape. And that black eye could be hiding a concussion."

June relented. "All right. Then?"

"Home. We both need sleep."

"What about Virginia Bridges?"

"Arrested. She's not going anywhere."

"You have her in custody?"

"Had her brought in for questioning when Brent took off with you. Gage said she's pitched a fit from the time he picked her up. I just called him and told him to arrest her on charges of first-degree murder. We'll get her arraigned tomorrow while the cadaver dog is going over this place. Then we'll question her about Hunter and all that he claimed here tonight."

"I want to be there."

Ray shook his head. "I can't let you question her."

"But I can watch."

"We'll talk about it." He tugged on her arm to turn her toward his cruiser.

June followed his lead, looking back at the Victorian. "What about—"

"Daniel will seal it off. It's not going anywhere."

He opened the door for her, but June paused, looking up at him. "Before you talk to Virginia, I need to give you a statement about what Brent Carter said. He knew. That Hunter would kill him."

"Are you sure?"

"He was just so…resigned to it. Defeated."

Ray motioned for her to get in. "I have a feeling that working with Hunter and Virginia Bridges would defeat even the strongest of men."

The visit to the E.R. didn't take as long as either of them expected. Fran Woodard and Nick Collins were on duty to take care of June's scrapes and bruises. Nick suspected some underlying injuries, however, and sent her off for X-rays and other diagnostic tests.

Ray took her statement while they waited for test results, growing ever more somber as she described each moment of the day. She watched his rage stoke in him, searing and dangerous but under control. After all these months, June recognized the signs clearly. The more dire a situation became, the more military he got on the outside—calm and controlled. Inside, however, he smoldered. His neck grew increasingly red, and every muscle tightened like hardening concrete. His eyes narrowed, but the light in them became as bright as a reflected diamond.

As he took down one of Brent's final statements, June reached out and put her hand on his arm. He looked up from his notepad, startled.

"What's wrong?"

She shook her head. "Nothing. But now is the time *you* need to listen to *me*."

"June—"

"Just listen, okay? Don't write. Just listen."

Ray lowered his pad. "Okay."

Her hand tightened on his forearm. "Brent felt he had no choice but to do what he did. He admired you, not them—"

"Then he shouldn't have—"

"Just listen!"

Ray's lips narrowed to a fine line. "Okay."

"When Hunter showed up, he was furious. I figured out pretty quick that Brent wasn't supposed to take me to Kentucky. He was supposed to take me back to the parsonage. He took me to the vacation house to stall, to get Hunter out of Virginia's range. He wanted to save us both. And if that didn't work, taking me across the state line meant you could call on the resources of the FBI.

"But none of it worked. Hunter had already started

down that 'I'm off my meds' act. He planned to use that to get out of everything. Even killing Brent."

"Now we can keep that from happening."

"And there's more. Brent died trying to save me."

Ray's features softened. "How so?"

"When Hunter couldn't be persuaded, Brent tried to arrest him. Hunter just laughed, walked over and punched him right in the face. Calm as I've ever seen someone do it. Brent wasn't prepared for that, and Hunter shot him with his own gun. That was Brent's gun he had in the attic."

Ray's shoulders dropped. "I see."

June took a deep breath, steeling herself for what she was about to say. "Ray, Brent's not the only one who admired you." She blinked twice, then continued. "Admires you. I do. More than you know."

"June, what you've been through is—"

She held up her hand. "*Please* let me finish before I lose my nerve." She swallowed hard, and he waited, eyebrows arched with curiosity. June plunged in, her words picking up speed with each one that came out of her mouth. "When I was going through all that, all I wanted was for you to be there. To be able to reach out and grab you and hold on for dear life. I vowed that if I ever saw you again, that's exactly what I'd do. I'd never turn my back and walk away from you again. I want to be with you. Always. I want to marry you, if you'll have me."

She stopped abruptly, holding her breath. Waiting. Watching.

Ray remained still a moment. "You're proposing to me."

"Yes."

"Now. In the middle of all this."

"We don't know how this will end, do we?"

Ray slowly put his pen back in his pocket, along with his notebook. He cupped her face in his hands. "June, my love, if I hadn't wanted to marry you, I sure wouldn't have hung on for the ride this long. You are, without a doubt, the best thing that's ever happened to me." He kissed her then, a soft, brief, loving kiss, a kiss to seal their love.

When he released her, June realized she was still holding her breath, and she gasped, filling her lungs. "So that's a yes?"

Ray laughed. "That would be a yes."

He started to kiss her again, but Nick chose that moment to return with the results. Ray stepped away from her quickly, and June took another deep breath. Then another, until Nick looked at her with suspicion. "Are you all right?"

She nodded vigorously. "More than you know." She glanced quickly at Ray, which prompted Nick to do the same. He looked at June again, then at Ray once more, studying their faces. Finally, he shook his head. "You two behave."

Ray grinned. "What's the verdict on the tests, Nick?"

"Pretty much what I expected. You took a hefty beating, but it's not as bad as it could have been." He went on to explain that June showed no evidence of a concussion, but the test revealed torn cartilage in one elbow and a hairline fracture in her hand. Despite both Nick's and Ray's questions, June couldn't remember exactly when they had occurred. Nick released her with a brace on her hand and instructions on taking care of her elbow.

When Ray pulled into her driveway, June looked pointedly at the sheriff's patrol car sitting across the street.

"I'm not taking any chances, June. Not till after they're arraigned and behind bars. I don't want you hurt again."

"I've had worse."

"Not on my watch."

"What about bail?"

He shook his head. "Not if we can make a case for first-degree murder. I talked to the D.A. while you were getting those tests done. He's confident we have the case on both. But we still don't know why they were so determined to steal or destroy David's hard drive, or what they think you knew about what was in that house. Until then, you could still be in danger."

June nodded. "Okay."

Ray got out and walked around to help her out of the cruiser. She took his arm as he escorted her to the door, leaning heavily against him. Once on her porch, Ray bent and kissed her lightly.

June smiled at him weakly, finally drained of her last ounce of energy. "I never want to say good-night without a kiss like that."

Ray chuckled. "I'll see what I can do."

He waited until June had locked herself inside the house. She walked through her home in darkness, too tired to even turn on a light. Without undressing, she eased onto her bed, kicked off her shoes and fell into a dreamless slumber.

The next day Ray arrived at the station refreshed and rested. He felt as if that morning's shower had removed a month of grime, and he'd slept better than he had in weeks. Only one more thing to conquer: bringing down Virginia Bridges.

He walked into the bullpen to find June already in a huddle with Jeff Gage.

"Both of you come with me." His hand on June's arm, he led them to the conference room, which had been locked overnight to protect the evidence still spread out on the table. He closed the door and turned first to Gage. "What about the cadaver dog?"

"The handler called about a half hour ago. She should be at the house—" he checked his watch "— in about ten minutes."

Ray nodded. "Good. Get over there and have them go over the grounds, the tunnel and the basement. Warn her about Kitty and David, so she knows not to let the dog get distracted."

"You got it."

"Then come back here. The D.A. is arraigning Virginia this morning, so they should be in front of the judge by nine-thirty or so. Then they'll be back here for questioning. Daniel has gone to NorthCrest to get Hunter's statement, and whatever Webster is willing to say."

June shifted her weight from one foot to the other. "What about me?"

Ray pointed at the evidence on the table. "I want you to go through the box of photos and the date book again, see if you find anything suspicious. Anything. Virginia is a formidable woman and a powerful lawyer. I want all our ducks in a row before I go in there to accuse her of first-degree murder."

"You think she'll try to get out of it?"

"I *know* she'll try to get out of it. Jeff, I also need the crime-scene photos of those shoe prints. I don't want anyone doubting that Virginia Bridges not only mastermined all this but was also on the scene."

Gage nodded and left the room, and Ray moved closer to June, touching her arm lightly. "You look disappointed."

She shrugged. "Not very exciting, going over evidence we've already examined."

"Catching the bad guys isn't always about trying to escape from a moving vehicle. Besides—" he pointed to a set of blinds at the end of the room "—that's one-way glass looking into the interrogation room where we're going to question Virginia."

June perked up. "Really?"

"Really. Just make sure the lights in here are off. And be quiet. If you have to talk, whisper."

He touched her cheek lightly, then left. *Time to beard the lion, Lord,* he prayed as he headed back to his office. *Give us all wisdom and strength.*

EIGHTEEN

Virginia Bridges had spent the night in jail, but when she paraded through the Bell County Sheriff's Department three hours later, she looked as if she had just returned from the salon. Her red power suit remained spotless and unwrinkled, and her still-ebony mane of hair was tucked neatly into a tight chignon. Her stiletto heels popped against the tile floor, like a herald announcing the arrival of a queen. Tall and lithe, she towered over most of the people in the room. At seventy-two, Virginia Bridges was the unmistakable matriarch of the county and not intimidated by anyone or anything, not even the threat of the death penalty.

As she entered the interrogation room with her entourage of a lawyer, a personal assistant and a stenographer, Ray stopped the D.A. at the rear of the crowd. "He gave her bail?"

The young prosecutor shrugged, his face pale with resignation. "She convinced the judge we didn't have a death-penalty case. Still, he made it one million. She posted right away."

Ray took a deep breath as he followed the crowd in. He was not looking forward to this.

Virginia sat primly in a chair on the far side of the table, and a dark-suited man sat next to her, setting a briefcase on the floor between their chairs. Virginia started without preamble.

"Sheriff Taylor, I will be representing myself. Mr. Morris will sit second chair, but please address your questions to me." She paused, waiting for the stenographer to get settled, then nodded at the prosecutor. "You, too, although I suspect you've not had time for Sheriff Taylor to bring you fully up to speed."

She folded her hands on the table. "However, before we begin, you might want to check with Deputy Rivers. He's at the hospital, is he not?"

The D.A.'s eyes popped wide. "How did you—"

Ray held up a hand to stop the prosecutor from letting his inexperience show any more than it already had, but he kept his eyes on Virginia. "Am I to assume he has news on this case?"

"He does. Despite the fact that Deputy Rivers went there to take Mr. Bridges's statement, you will find that my son is no longer in a position to offer any testimony against me. His wild claims obviously were made under duress. He was in the throes of the most severe side effects of withdrawing from some powerful antipsychotic drugs. His statements won't be admissible in court. Mr. Webster also will be unavailable for testimony."

She leaned forward, just enough to emphasize the

power of her next statement. "Without them, Sheriff Taylor, you have not one shred of direct physical evidence connecting me to any of the crimes I'm supposed to have committed or masterminded. And by the time I get through with a jury, they will see me as a simple and caring mother taken advantage of by a powerful but mentally ill son. Tragic, but definitely not criminal."

Ray's cell phone chirped, signaling an incoming text message, but he ignored it as he stared at Virginia Bridges, forming his response in his head.

She motioned toward the phone, a smug smile settling on her face. "You should take that. It's Deputy Rivers calling from the hospital."

Curious in spite of himself, Ray looked. The message was simple:

D.R. 911

"No one say anything else," Ray commanded, then stood and left the room.

"I really, really despise her."

Peering over June's left shoulder, Jeff Gage agreed. "Lots to despise."

"Wonder what changed Hunter's and Webster's minds?"

"Money, probably." He stepped away and looked back at the evidence on the table. "Are you sure you didn't find anything?"

"Nothing. Nada. What about the cadaver dog?"

He shook his head. "The handler did a quick survey with him, but he didn't pick up anything. She said she'd go over every inch more carefully, then call me if she found anything."

June shoved one of the chairs up under the table. "There has to be something here." She picked up JR's date book, waggling it in frustration. She stopped, staring at it, and shook it again. It felt stiff in her hand, the back of it particularly unyielding.

Gage watched her for a moment. "What's wrong?"

She looked up at him, puzzled. "JR always bought leather date books. The cover on this should flop like an overused Bible."

"Maybe something's stuck to the cover."

June opened the date book and examined the back cover. Nothing stuck to it, but it still had an unusual inflexibility. She laid it flat on the table and pressed two fingers down on it at the top, the middle and the bottom. "Definitely something in there." She looked at Gage. "Do you have a pocket knife?"

He reached into his pocket, but stopped when the door slammed open, banging into the wall. Ray stormed in, growling, pausing to sling his cell phone across the room.

June and Gage froze. "Ray?" she asked quietly.

"She tried to get them killed!" Ray turned and hit the wall with his open hand, so hard the thud echoed around the room.

"What?"

He turned and looked at them, his face a stormy mask of fury. "Hunter Bridges and Stephen Webster." He pointed at the demolished cell phone. "That was

Rivers. The whole hospital is in chaos. The Springfield police are all over, and they're calling in the TBI. On my watch."

"What happened?" asked Gage.

Ray shook his head. "They don't know yet. Sometime during this morning's shift change, they had four patients crash within a few minutes of each other, including Bridges and Webster. I'm going to kill her." He started toward the door.

"Ray—"

He pointed a finger at her as he headed out. "Stay out of this, June."

June and Gage watched him go in stunned silence. After a moment, June moved first, turning back toward the young deputy. "Give me that knife."

Gage pulled it from his pocket and opened the largest blade. June took it, slipping the tip between the layers of leather at the bottom of the rear cover. They separated slowly, and June pulled one up so that she could get her fingers in the opening. Pinching the edge of a hard surface, June pulled, easing a computer disk out of the date book.

It was labeled simply "Insurance." They stared at it a moment, then both of them sprinted for Jeff Gage's computer.

Ray hesitated outside the interrogation room long enough to regain his bearings. He had faced evil a number of times in his life but never like this. Never in the form of a composed and sophisticated woman, a woman who had tried to murder her own child.

Virginia looked at him with a hard stare but said nothing.

"You tried to kill your own son to cover up your involvement in murder," he continued.

"That's the difference between your interrogation and my day in court. You have theories. I have the facts." She glanced at Mr. Morris, who picked up the briefcase and removed several blue-backed documents.

Virginia continued. "For instance, I have affidavits verifying my alibis. Quite simply, I was somewhere else when all these tragic events occurred. I have a copy of the police report on my stolen convertible." She paused, smiling slightly at Ray. "Which, by the way, we will be suing your department for destroying."

Ray opened his mouth to ask a question when the door behind him popped open and June was suddenly at his side with a set of papers in hand. "Look at these," she insisted.

Ray looked up at June, irritated, an emotion that was aggravated when Virginia spoke sharply.

"Quite inappropriate for JR Eaton's tramp wife to be in here. She is your only other suspect, is she not?"

They both ignored her, but Ray glared at June. "Get out, June."

She shook her head, jabbing her finger at the papers she'd laid on the table.

Puzzled, Ray glanced down. When he saw the document on top, his eyes widened and he looked back up at June. "Where did you get this?"

She held up the disk. "It was concealed in JR's date book. The papers he promised to destroy. He did destroy them. But he didn't get rid of them. He scanned them. They're all on the disk."

"What is it?" asked the D.A.

June looked up at him, then at Virginia, then back at Ray. "It's a list of bribes. Local, state, national. Judges, senators, lobbyists. The disk also holds the paper trails to back up the list. Bank accounts, some offshore. And more. Lots more. A trail of corruption that dates back to the eighties."

Virginia stood up, fully indignant. "You can't possibly have—"

June turned on her. "Thanks to your son, Virginia. There's a note on one of the files. Hunter gave all this to JR to protect himself. He knew how dangerous you were. He even feared you'd resort to murder if things didn't go your way."

June leaned over the table, glaring at Virginia. "Do you have any idea what it's like for a child to know his own mother could kill him? I hope they put you under the jail and let you rot there!"

Virginia's cold response targeted Ray. "Get her out of here!"

Ray stood, somewhat ashamed at how much he was enjoying this moment. "Surely you're not bothered by the accusations of the woman you called 'JR Eaton's tramp wife.'"

The D.A. crossed his arms. "Personally, I'd like to see Mrs. Bridges left in a room alone with June for about fifteen minutes. I think it would spare the county the expense of a trial."

"This is outrageous. We're leaving." Virginia started around the table, leaving Mr. Morris to scramble to his feet.

Ray blocked her path, facing her eye to eye. "I don't think so."

"You have no right to stop me. I'm out on bail."

"For murder. You're now under arrest for soliciting a bribe and conspiring to defraud. Turn around."

"I will not submit to this ludicrous—"

"Turn around!" Ray's tone left no doubt in anyone's mind who was in charge. Including Virginia Bridges. Slowly and without any loss of dignity, she turned her back on him, allowing him to handcuff her.

"I can take it from here," murmured the D.A.

Ray nodded. "One of my officers will help you."

He watched as the prosecutor and a deputy escorted Virginia Bridges and her team from the station, then slid his arm around June.

She took a deep breath. "Is it wrong to say how much I enjoyed that?"

Ray shook his head as he gazed down at her. "No. It should always feel good to save the day. And you did. I'm proud of you."

"Thank you, Ray. That means the world to me. So. Do you think things will calm down now?"

Ray kissed the top of her head. "No."

"No? What do you mean?" June asked, looking concerned.

"Well," he replied, "you have a wedding to plan, after all."

EPILOGUE

In typical June fashion, the wedding came together almost overnight. She found an open date on the church calendar, booked it, then engaged a wedding planner who handled everything from the invitations to the catering. She found a dress on sale at a shop in Nashville and used the same store for the bridesmaids' dresses. Within two weeks, she'd completed all the arrangements.

The biggest decision about the wedding, however, didn't involve any of the arrangements. After an emotional discussion with April, June stepped out on a limb and invited their sister, Lindsey, who'd been estranged from them since their mother had died. Being with Ray, and enduring what they'd just been through, made June desire to bring what was left of her family back together. June said a little prayer the day she dropped the invitation in the mail, leaving the rest to God...

...who, of course, came through. June actually squealed when Lindsey accepted the wedding invitation, even offering to help cater it. June, who had her own plans, insisted on Lindsey being in the wedding party, intentionally pairing her with Deputy Jeff Gage.

When that bright summer day dawned, June met Ray, resplendent in his dress uniform, at the altar of White Hills Gospel Immanuel Chapel. She couldn't remember ever being quite as happy as the moment they retreated down the aisle, arm in arm, and headed for the reception, which was set up on the lawn of the freshly repaired Victorian parsonage.

June, the train of her dress looped up over one arm, flitted from one cluster of guests to another. As if she'd just awakened from a three-year-long sleep, June embraced her new future with grace and enthusiasm. Ray stayed mostly with a group of his deputies, but June knew all too well that he seldom took his eyes off her the whole day, sending a radiant beam of joy through her entire being.

June, determined to spread the wealth on her wedding day, found repeated reasons to throw her arms around Jeff Gage and Lindsey, until Lindsey, laughing, whispered in her ear, "Do you want me to get to know him or not?" Grinning, June squeezed her one last time and stepped away, leaving her younger sister alone with the deputy.

Adjusting the train of her dress again, June turned back toward the house. When an unknown guest caught her eye, however, the flitting bride came to a complete halt. June watched the woman closely. Tall, willowy and blonde, the elegant lady in her early fifties picked up a cup of punch from the end of the reception table and stood silently, gazing up at the Victorian with a strange look in her eyes.

June's brows furrowed as she focused on the newcomer, a total stranger who looked incredibly familiar. Recognition came slowly, and June's mouth went slack as she realized that the last time she'd seen that face had been in a photo. A photo of Rosalie Osborne, with her father, Montgomery, seated in a wheelchair beside her. It was the same jawline, the same brow, the same wide-set, gorgeous blue eyes.

June approached her slowly, as if the woman were a dream or a skittish wild animal that would bolt when she saw June. Instead, when the woman shifted her gaze, she smiled and offered her hand. "You must be June Eaton."

June took her hand, shaking it firmly. "Taylor, actually. June Taylor."

The woman laughed. "Of course. Congratulations. I hear he's a good man."

"Thank you. He is. More than most." June cleared her throat. "I don't believe we've met?"

"No. I'm Katrina. Katrina Lincoln. I'm sorry to crash your wedding, but I'm only in town for a day or so, and I'd heard how hard you and your first husband had worked to restore this house. I had to see it."

June tried to play coy, even though she knew coy didn't suit her very well. "Oh? Are you from around here?"

Katrina turned back to the house, her eyes glowing with admiration and affection. "You did a tremendous job on the house. She always was a glorious painted lady. You gave her what she deserved."

"It was a labor of love."

Katrina looked down at the ground a moment, then up at June. "I hear the local library will take her over now. Is that right?"

"Yes. We finally located Rosalie Osborne's will. The church is going to honor it and turn the house over. The library plans to use it for their administrative offices and county archives."

"Excellent choice." Katrina hesitated, and her voice dropped. "So people around here have finally accepted that she's dead."

June considered her answer carefully, watching the woman next to her intently. "Or at least that Rosalie's gone for good. Never to return."

A faint smile played around the corners of Katrina's mouth. "Well, it *is* a name I've not heard in a long time."

"I suspect not since 1986."

"Indeed." Katrina took a deep breath, looked at the house one more time, then turned to face June. "I'm glad it was you, June."

"Me, too."

The other woman nodded, then backed away a few steps. "I live in Chicago now. Great city. Easy to get lost in." She continued backward a few more steps. "If you ever get lost there, look me up. I'm really not that hard to find." She raised a hand in farewell, then turned away, strolling to a green BMW convertible. June watched as she tucked herself neatly behind the wheel, lowered the tan roof and backed out into the street. Katrina waved one last time, just before she turned the street corner, disappearing again.

June continued to stare until she felt the warm, comfortable presence of her husband behind her. Ray rested his hands on her waist and pulled her against his chest. "Who was that?"

"Katrina Lincoln."

"I don't know her."

"No one does. I don't think anyone ever did."

"Today, my love, is not the day to turn cryptic on me."

A laugh burst from June, and she turned, sliding her arms around his neck and focusing all her attention on him. "I'll explain later. Until then, you know what I want?"

"Something that involves me, I hope."

She grinned. "I want you to pick me up and whisk me off home. No big goodbyes. No rice throwing. Let's just disappear."

"People will talk."

"Won't be the first time. Won't be the last. Let them. We'll know the truth."

"Which is?"

Her hold on him tightened. "That what God brings together, not even gossip can tear apart."

Ray Taylor laughed, then scooped his wife up in his arms and walked away with her, heading for their new life.

* * * * *

Dear Reader,

June Presley Eaton Taylor is one of the more unique heroines I've ever written about. She's feisty and outspoken, but with a past that has made her doubt herself as well as God's love for her. June is a widow, and her first husband, JR, pulled her from a life on the streets and led her to God. In her mind, JR's love for her was directly tied to God's love for her, and she has a hard time separating them. In many ways, she can't quite believe God would love her just for who she is. Just for being June.

I can relate, as I know some of you can. When we think about all the unloving, "unchristian" things we may have done in our lives, it's hard to believe that God loves us anyway.

But God's grace and salvation are not about our actions; they're about His love. When we accept Jesus as our Savior, God adopts us into His family, no matter what our past. As a result, He never intends us to live in fear. We are to live in love as His beloved children. You. Me. All of us.

I hope you enjoy June's journey, as she discovers that most glorious truth.

Blessings,

Ramona

QUESTIONS FOR DISCUSSION

1. In what ways can you identify with June? With Ray?

2. June had gone to confront David Gallagher about his implication that she supported a man she detested. Have people ever thought you held a belief you did not? How did you feel about this? What steps did you take to change their minds?

3. The book opens with a scripture passage from Romans 8. Which characters in the book struggle most with a "spirit of fear," fighting to remind themselves that we are all children of God?

4. For much of the book, June's identity is still woven around her marriage to JR. Have you ever had a similar connection to a past relationship?

5. If you could talk to June, what advice would you have given her about her belief that a new love would mean betraying JR?

6. What does the Corvette represent for June? For Ray? In what way does its destruction change June's feelings toward both men? Have you ever had an equally strong attachment to a gift from a

loved one? Why do you think such symbols create powerful emotions within us?

7. Why do you think June has a harder time accepting a new relationship than Ray does?

8. How would you describe the difference between Ray's relationship with Anne and June's with JR?

9. How do you feel about Ray's willingness to wait for June? Why do you think the events in the book make him finally push her a bit to see what's happening around her?

10. In what ways does the Victorian home that JR and June renovated represent their relationship?

11. What does June's reaction to Ray being shot reveal about her feelings toward him? How does this show that her attitude may be changing?

12. Whose faith do you think is stronger? Which actions in the book reveal the strength of Ray's and June's relationship with God?

13. Ray feels he needs more strength and wisdom from God to confront Virginia Bridges than her son. Why do you think he feels this way? In what way is Virginia the more difficult opponent?

14. How do you feel about June's final statement, "That what God brings together, not even gossip can tear apart"? What change in June does it represent?

15. Did you like the ending? Why or why not?

INSPIRATIONAL

Inspirational romances to warm your heart & soul.

TITLES AVAILABLE NEXT MONTH

Available May 10, 2011

UNDERCOVER PURSUIT
Missions of Mercy
Susan May Warren

THREAT OF EXPOSURE
Texas Ranger Justice
Lynette Eason

THE OFFICER'S SECRET
Military Investigations
Debby Giusti

WITNESS ON THE RUN
Hope White

LISCNM0411

REQUEST YOUR FREE BOOKS!

2 FREE RIVETING INSPIRATIONAL NOVELS
PLUS 2 FREE MYSTERY GIFTS

Love Inspired®
SUSPENSE

YES! Please send me 2 FREE Love Inspired® Suspense novels and my 2 FREE mystery gifts (gifts are worth about $10). After receiving them, if I don't wish to receive any more books, I can return the shipping statement marked "cancel". If I don't cancel, I will receive 4 brand-new novels every month and be billed just $4.24 per book in the U.S. or $4.74 per book in Canada. That's a saving of at least 23% off the cover price. It's quite a bargain! Shipping and handling is just 50¢ per book in the U.S. and 75¢ per book in Canada.* I understand that accepting the 2 free books and gifts places me under no obligation to buy anything. I can always return a shipment and cancel at any time. Even if I never buy another book, the two free books and gifts are mine to keep forever.

123/323 IDN FDCT

Name _____ (PLEASE PRINT)

Address _____ Apt. #

City _____ State/Prov. _____ Zip/Postal Code

Signature (if under 18, a parent or guardian must sign)

Mail to the **Reader Service:**
IN U.S.A.: P.O. Box 1867, Buffalo, NY 14240-1867
IN CANADA: P.O. Box 609, Fort Erie, Ontario L2A 5X3

Not valid for current subscribers to Love Inspired Suspense books.

**Are you a subscriber to Love Inspired Suspense
and want to receive the larger-print edition?
Call 1-800-873-8635 or visit www.ReaderService.com.**

* Terms and prices subject to change without notice. Prices do not include applicable taxes. Sales tax applicable in N.Y. Canadian residents will be charged applicable taxes. Offer not valid in Quebec. This offer is limited to one order per household. All orders subject to credit approval. Credit or debit balances in a customer's account(s) may be offset by any other outstanding balance owed by or to the customer. Please allow 4 to 6 weeks for delivery. Offer available while quantities last.

Your Privacy—The Reader Service is committed to protecting your privacy. Our Privacy Policy is available online at www.ReaderService.com or upon request from the Reader Service.

We make a portion of our mailing list available to reputable third parties that offer products we believe may interest you. If you prefer that we not exchange your name with third parties, or if you wish to clarify or modify your communication preferences, please visit us at www.ReaderService.com/consumerchoice or write to us at Reader Service Preference Service, P.O. Box 9062, Buffalo, NY 14269. Include your complete name and address.

LISUS11

Love Inspired **HISTORICAL**

Save $1.00 when you purchase
2 or more Love Inspired® Historical books.

SAVE
$1.00

when you purchase 2 or more
Love Inspired® Historical books.

Coupon expires September 30, 2011. Redeemable at participating retail outlets in the U.S. and Canada only. Limit one coupon per customer.

52609783

5 65373 00076 2   (8100)0 11736

LIHCOUPON1

Love Inspired

Miriam Yoder always thought she'd marry her neighbor, a good dependable man. But then local veterinarian John Hartman catches her eye, a handsome, charming man who is not Plain. Miriam is confused, but must listen to her heart to truly know which man will claim her love and her future.

Miriam's Heart
by Emma Miller

✦ Hannah's ✦
Daughters

*Available May
wherever books are sold.*